Pie In The Sky

Garth Wallace

Laughter forever!
Garth

Published By

Happy Landings

Other books by Garth Wallace

Fly Yellow Side Up
Blue Collar Pilots
Don't Call Me a Legend
Derry Air

Canadian Catalogue Data

PIE IN THE SKY

fiction, humor, aviation

first printing, 1993
second printing, 1998

Written by Garth Wallace, 1946 -

ISBN 0-9697322-0-1

C813'.54

Editing: **Liz Wallace**
     Sari Funston

Cover Design: **Dave Robertson**

Cover Art: **Andy Cienick**

Layout and Typesetting: **Amadeo Gaspar**

Written and produced in Canada

Published by: **Happy Landings**
     RR # 4
     Merrickville, Ontario
     Canada, K0G 1N0

     Tel.: 613-269-2552
     Fax: 613-269-3962
     Web site: www.happylanding.com
     E-mail: books@happylanding.com

Contents

Introduction

This book is classified as fiction, but don't believe it. I didn't invent airplanes, laughter, frost, sightseeing flights, or school crossing guards — they already existed. The people and events in Pie In The Sky are composites of real personalities and experiences in aviation. The names have been changed to protect the guilty. You may feel you know them. Interesting characters and funny stories are everywhere in aviation. Enjoy them as I have.

Garth Wallace

1/ Welcome to Pie

What I saw when I pulled into the flying school parking lot did not improve my state of mind. Pie Municipal Airport appeared to hold little promise for work. There were two buildings — a large, old wooden hangar and a small, brick office. I could see three garden-variety Cessna airplanes and a well-worn Piper Colt parked on the ramp. There were a few other aircraft in tie-downs and three cars in the lot, but the sky was empty. It was like a scene from a doomsday movie. Nothing was moving, even the windsock hung limp on its ring.

The sleepy scene was typical of many small-town airports in Canada. The field was probably left over from the war and was now being operated by a few aviation diehards who had more enthusiasm than business sense.

No people and no flying could only mean no job. I pushed myself to get out of my Volkswagen Beetle and look around anyway. I walked over to the brick "terminal building" and opened the door. Inside was a livingroom-sized lounge with large windows overlooking the runways. A counter along the right side provided a divider for an office. A man with his back to me was leaning on the counter and talking to a young woman on the other side. When I closed the door he stopped in mid-sentence and turned my way. He seemed surprised to see a stranger.

"Can I help you?" he asked. His tone indicated that I must be lost.

He was a tall man in his late twenties. Baggy clothes gave him a clown-like, shapeless appearance. His long, horse face was topped with an unruly shock of red hair. I decided he must be the janitor or maybe a mechanic.

"Is the manager around?" I asked politely.

His face lit up. "That's me," he declared with a big smile.

The reply surprised me, but I recovered quickly and introduced myself. "I'm a flying instructor who has just moved into town and I'm looking for work."

His body jerked into motion almost like a child's wind-up toy. He lurched toward me with his grin widening and his head bobbing up and down. Instead of shaking my hand, he took my shoulders in both hands. "Can you start today?" He boomed the question in my face. At the same time he nodded his own head up and down again, as if forcing me to say, "Yes."

"Sure," I said. It was a startled, automatic response.

"That's fantastic," he roared, "you can fly with my first student." He was getting very excited. He held my shoulders as if to prevent me from changing my mind.

"You came at the perfect time," he continued. "The student will be here soon and it's his first flying lesson. I really hate giving those." He released one shoulder so he could pump my hand. "I'm Hector Smithers," he said, calming slightly. "and this here's our receptionist, Ursula." He waved toward the girl. She smiled and nodded.

"This is great," he added, turning excited again. Then he looked at his watch. "Well, you'll be flying TWX, the red and white Cessna One-Fifty out there. You'd better go and check it over. Ursula will introduce you to the customer when he gets here." The girl smiled again.

"I'm going to call my folks," Smithers continued, "I want to take them flying."

He pushed me toward the door and turned to the phone.

My mind was well behind what was going on, but I collected myself. Halfway to the door I stopped.

"Excuse me, Hector," I said, almost apologetically, "I have very little time in Cessna 150s. I've been flying floatplanes for the last six months. Shouldn't I have a checkout first?"

The checkout was just one of the thoughts rushing into my head — what about salary, schedule, curriculum? The manager/janitor's reaction to my job request was unexpected and bizarre. It didn't seem right.

"Nonsense," Hector said, looking at his watch again, "if you've flown on wheels, you never forget — like riding a bike. You have flown on wheels, haven't you?"

"Yes sir."

"Well, there you go. And Cessna 150s are the easiest airplanes in the world to fly."

I was forming an unflattering character assessment of this man. What sort of manager would hire an instructor off the street and send him flying, knowing nothing more than his name? He hadn't checked my pilot licence, log book or background, but I was also making up my mind to take the job. It was here and it was now. I could always quit if I found something better. In the meantime, I could learn the school's regulations and curriculum from the chief flying instructor.

Hector mistook my hesitation as a possible change of heart. He scurried over and put a hand on my shoulder. "What level instructor rating do you have?" he asked.

"Class Two," I replied.

My answer made him excited again. "That's great. I'll give you a raise. You can be the chief flying instructor!" He was almost jumping up and down. "I don't like that part of my job, there's too much paperwork." He seemed as happy as I was bewildered.

"There, it's all settled. Welcome to Pie In the Sky Flying School," he said, pumping my hand again. "Now, check the airplane over and I'll talk to you later. I'm going to take my folks for a ride in the Cessna One-Seventy-Two. We just got it today."

I stood there with my mouth open. Five minutes on the job and already I was the CFI. Now I definitely wanted to know more about the operation, but Hector was already dialing the phone. He smiled and shooed me out the door with his hand. I closed my mouth and walked to the airplane.

For many good reasons I felt like I was riding an emotional roller coaster. The past summer had been fantastic. I had worked a dream job as a bush pilot in Paradise, a small town in the heart of Central Ontario's vacationland. Fire patrols, fishing charters, floatplane flying lessons, emergency medical flights — I had done it all. It had been rich and rewarding. There is nothing in aviation that matches the fantastic feeling of freedom that comes with flying over a carpet of clear lakes and being able to land on any one of them.

And the people had been great. The air service's woodsy customers had character — forest rangers, fishermen, cottagers — and they had become my good friends. The bush airplanes had personalities — the Beaver, the Found, the Super Cub — and they had treated me well.

But then came autumn. The work grew scarce, the daylight shortened and my paycheck dwindled. Rich and rewarding turned into cold, dark and bleak.

My wife Susan and I decided to look for jobs elsewhere. I had a commercial pilot licence and a flying instructor's rating. I didn't have much hope of finding a flying job in November, but Susan had a background in retailing ladies wear. We would move to wherever we could find work.

Susan won. Through an old acquaintance she landed the assistant manager's job at a new ladies' clothing store in Pie, a small town in southwestern Ontario. We loaded our Volkswagen Beetle with dog and belongings and bid goodbye to the bush.

Pie In The Sky

We discovered that Pie was a tidy commercial centre serving the tobacco farming in the area. Most of the businesses were strung out on either side of one long main street. The houses and storefronts were perfectly uninteresting. To outsiders like us it looked like Anywhere, Canada, a false-front town built on a movie lot. It didn't help that we didn't know anyone in Pie. The people held the same anonymity as the buildings.

On our first full day in town I had driven Susan to her new job and headed for the local airport. I had no job and was being supported by my wife. It was a low point in my life and it bothered me. Susan was being good about it, but I wasn't.

Going from that to being hired as a flying instructor and then being promoted to chief instructor, all in five minutes, was a mental whiplashing. I didn't know whether to whoop or worry.

Some of my uncertainty subsided when I saw TWX. The Cessna 150 was nearly new. The paint wasn't chipped, the windshield was clear, the instruments were readable and there was carpet. Most small town flying schools could not afford the luxury of new aircraft. It was a special treat after a season of flying battered, old bush planes reeking of fish guts and moose quarters.

I checked the gas and oil, and then sat in the pilot's seat enjoying the smell of the new plane. This job might not be too bad. Except for the odd name of the place and the manager who must have been born under a full moon, there had to be something right about a flying school with new airplanes.

2/ The Brown Baron

The young college student riding beside me suddenly twitched in his seat. It was the involuntary start people do when they catch something unexpected out of the corner of their eye. I leaned forward to follow his line of sight.

Another small airplane was approaching from the right. It was on a converging course, but still some distance away. My student, Phil Patterson, watched the aircraft, obviously fascinated to see another machine suspended in the air.

As the intruder grew larger, I recognized it as the new brown and yellow Cessna 172 from the flying school. It was the airplane that the manager, Hector Smithers, had said he was going to use to take his family for a ride. That had been an hour ago. In that hour, I'd gone from unemployed bush pilot to chief flying instructor of the Pie In The Sky Flying School. In the process Hector had assigned me to teach Phil so he could fly with his family in the new airplane.

Meeting Hector in the sky provided a welcome break. As Phil watched him angle closer, I collected my thoughts. I'd been struggling with the lesson. The Cessna 150 was unfamiliar and I hadn't done much teaching lately. I drew a deep breath and relaxed for a moment. Instructing on wheels made me feel like a fish out of water after spending the summer bush flying, but I was glad to have the job. I knew I would settle down after spending time in the aircraft. It would help when I learned more about the Pie In The Sky operation.

Phil Patterson was a young, macho guy from the local college. This was his first flying lesson. I took advantage of the encounter with Hector.

"You see it's important to keep an eye out for traffic," I said.

As I spoke, the other Cessna suddenly pushed over into a steep dive. Phil and I both leaned forward to watch it descend.

"What's he doing?" Phil asked in a surprised voice. The airplane was about to disappear below our nose.

"I have no idea," I said truthfully. The abruptness of the dive was unusual for a family-type airplane. It was a stunt pilot manoeuver.

As soon as I answered, the airplane reversed its death drop and started pitching up, rotating into a climb. It crossed our horizon going straight up and continued pitching onto its back, completing a loop. Hector was flying an airshow, and Phil and I were in the front row.

Phil turned to me and said, "I didn't think you could do aerobatics in these airplanes."

"You can't, unless you're really careful," I said. I wasn't being completely truthful, but I didn't want to explain why our flying school manager was illegally stunting an airplane.

The 172 wasn't close enough to see who was inside, so I decided that Hector's family must have been unavailable. He must have gone up on his own. The Cessna wasn't designed for aerobatics, but a smoothly-executed loop with a light load wouldn't hurt it. I admired Hector's skill. It changed my first impression of him.

Hector's show wasn't over. With the speed gathered from the back of the loop, he pitched the airplane into a barrel roll, ending with a shallow dive. Then he pulled the Cessna straight up and held it there. Before the airplane's momentum completely died, he kicked it into a stall turn and dove underneath us, heading in the opposite direction. I don't think he ever saw us. I banked our airplane slightly to the right so we could keep him in sight. Hector continued flying straight away from us.

Phil looked at me, anticipating a further explanation. I didn't have one. I couldn't tell him we had witnessed the flying school manager breaking air regulations. I ignored his quizzical expression and started back into the lesson. While demonstrating the basic control movements and airplane attitudes, I watched for the Brown Baron, but he didn't return.

Back on the ground, I completed a post-flight briefing with Phil. He asked a few questions, but didn't mention the airshow again. I showed him how to fill in his pilot log and booked his next lesson.

Phil left and the Cessna 172 taxied in from the runway. It seemed to sit a little tail low, but was otherwise intact. I looked a little closer. I couldn't believe my eyes. The airplane was full. Apparently Hector's family had gone with him.

I watched as the flying school manager opened the door and hopped down from the pilot's seat. A women I guessed to be Hector's wife, climbed out from the other front seat with a baby in her arms. An older woman handed Hector a youngster who had been riding on her lap in the back. Then she heaved her considerable bulk from the airplane. An older man squeezed out of the other side of the back seat. He was bigger still.

Hector had stunted the four-place Cessna with six people on

board. The fact that he had flown it overloaded was bad enough. It was a miracle that he hadn't pulled the airplane apart doing aerobatics. I thought I had seen it all working for a bush operator, but none of the shinanigans up north compared to what Hector had done. I obviously had a lot to learn about this operation.

His family seemed none the worse for their wild ride. I had flown for nearly an hour after they had disappeared from view. For all I knew, they had been upside down for much of that time. But they were all smiling and no one was kissing the ground or carrying a little white bag.

As Hector walked toward the office, I was riding mixed emotions. I had landed a new job which I should quit after seeing my boss trying to disassemble one of the airplanes in the air. I wasn't sure how to handle this.

"Hi. How'd it go with your first student?" Hector asked cheerfully.

"Fine," I lied.

"Great. You're probably wondering about your pay and things," he said, handing the airplane's log book to Ursula. "We can work that out soon enough, but I have three more students for you this afternoon."

Hector started toward the door. If I was going to address the stunting problem, I had to speak now or never. "Before you go Hector, could I talk to you about one thing?"

"Sure, shoot," he said, stopping in the middle of the lounge.

"I'm a little concerned about what I saw you do in the 172," I said tentatively.

"What'd you see that bothered you?" he asked. He didn't seem concerned. "Was it flying under the wires at Uncle Ernie's house, chasing the motorboat on Lake Erie, or the touch and go landing we did on Highway 401?"

It wasn't the reaction I was expecting. "Actually I was thinking of the aerobatics," I replied.

"The aerobatics? Shucks, we do those all the time. Heck, Mom wouldn't go up again if I didn't fly her upside down a couple of times. But if you don't like it, you could fire me. You're the CFI, remember?"

His big grin made it hard to take him seriously. Before I could say anything, he answered for me.

"Consider me fired. Now as manager, I'll hire me back again," he said with a laugh. "Is there anything else?"

A clown; I was working for a guy who dressed and talked like a clown and who flew like Chuck Yeager. "No, that's all," I said.

"Good," he said, patting me on the shoulder, "I'll see you later. Welcome to Pie In The Sky."

11

3/ Whoa

Hector disappeared in the direction of the hangar, leaving me to fly with his students. It was like learning to swim in the deep end with no instructions. Ursula Bognar, the receptionist, tried to be helpful. She gave me the files and log book of each student before they came in, but the files contained no records of previous lessons or instructor comments. I had to ask the students where they were on the course.

It was a busy afternoon, but I did get a chance to look around in the air. I could see that the Pie Airport was just four kilometres west of town. The surrounding farms lay in neat brown rows of freshly-plowed land. Two rail lines entered the town at 90 degrees to each other and crossed in the middle. A spur line joined them in a gentle bend. The town had grown from the "pie" of land between the tracks.

The Pie Airport was one of many in Canada built during World War II for the Commonwealth Air Training Plan. They were all the same, a pie-shaped triangular layout of three, half-mile long runways. It was a clear day and it was easy to see why southern Ontario was picked for a large concentration of those CATP bases. The land was flat and the climate was good. There was nothing for a pilot to run into higher than the water tower in town. The mid-November temperature was above zero and the sky was clear. It would be easy to like this area.

When I finished with my last student, it was dark. The office was open, the lights were on, but Ursula had gone home. She had left the customer's bill on the counter. I felt abandoned. The airplanes were still out and there seemed to be no one around. I finished with the student and was thinking of following him out the door when Hector appeared from the hangar.

"Hi, how'd it go?" he asked.

"Fine," I said, "I thought everyone had gone and left me."

"No, no," he said with a laugh. "A manager's job is never done. I was working in the hangar. Come on, I'll help you put the airplanes away."

"Sure," I said. I was hoping this was my opportunity to find out more about the place.

Walking out the door, Hector said, "Yes sir, it's been a good day. I'm glad you came along."

"Thank you, it's good to be working," I replied, telepathing a salary request.

"Tomorrow, you'll meet Roger, the other instructor," Hector continued. "You fly with my students again and I'll take a badly-needed day off."

"Sure," I replied. Hector didn't get my message.

We walked toward the flying school's four airplanes parked on the ramp. I thought we were going to pull them the short distance to the hangar, but Hector climbed into the new Cessna 172 and started it up. I walked over to the nearest Cessna 150.

The hangar was a monstrous old wooden one left over from World War II. It stood next to the brick terminal building that held the school office and lounge. Hector taxied to the hangar and continued to drive the aircraft inside, turning it around in a half circle before shutting down. There was room to pull in and turn behind him, but the thought of operating an airplane's whirling propeller and 10-metre wingspan in the confines of a building was too intimidating. I stopped in front of the hangar.

Hector walked over while I was getting out. "What's the matter," he asked. "I left lots of room, didn't I?"

"I've never taxied into a hangar before," I said.

"Oh, we always drive them in," he said, helping me pull the Cessna. "There's lots of room and running them inside blows the floor clean."

"Okay," I said, "you're the boss."

I looked around. Filling the back half of the building were four prehistoric-looking, mechanical monsters. Each had a large oil-oozing radial engine hung on its nose and wings rotated 90 degrees and folded along fat fuselages. They sat rearing back on tail-wheel type landing gear. I had never seen them before.

"What are those?" I asked.

Hector's face lit up. "Grumman Avengers," he replied with a big smile. "The military called them TBMs."

I followed him over to the nearest one. Standing underneath the aircraft, I could just touch its belly at the wing root, but I didn't. The layers of faded red, yellow and orange paint were streaked with oil, gas, exhaust and chemicals.

"They were carrier-based torpedo bombers in World War II," Hector continued. "We use them for aerial spraying and water bombing. I'm going to fly one next spring." He was really beaming.

I failed to see the source of his pride. The Avengers carried the scars of 25 years of agricultural combat. Their appearance wasn't helped by the fact they were in various stages of off-season repair. But Hector stood smiling under the chemical-crusted monster as if it was the latest fighter plane. I smiled agreeably and made a mental note to remember that the Avengers were his favourite subject.

The building also contained the rest of the Pie In The Sky fleet — two Piper Pawnees — small, single-seat agricultural airplanes. They were parked in a corner along with the usual assortment of clutter that accummulates in old hangars — broken boats, broken towbars, an old Herman-Nelson heater and a homemade house trailer.

We walked around to the ramp for the two remaining aircraft. Hector climbed into the other new 150, so I headed for the old Piper Colt. The Colt and the Cessna 150 are both two-place, tricycle-geared, high-wing trainers with about 100 horsepower, but there the similarity ended. The Cessna was a modern, clean-looking, all-metal aircraft. The Piper was a throw-back to the 1930's when airplanes were made with welded tubing and covered with cloth. The Colt's numerous struts, bracing wires and external control cables were a flying contradiction to modern aerodynamics.

I pulled myself into the airplane using the steel tubes that crisscrossed the interior. I had flown a Colt before, so I had no trouble finding the switches and controls. The airplane started easily and moved right away.

Even with the throttle pulled all the way back, I was heading for the hangar opening at a good clip. I reached for the brake. The Colt's token brakes consisted of a single lever hanging from under the instrument panel attached to a puny master cylinder on the floor by a limp cable. I pulled. The brakes offered about the same resistance as dragging my foot on the ramp. The airplane charged into the hanger without slowing down. I was quickly plunged into a bad situation.

My choices were simple — continue into the torpedo bomber parked straight ahead, or turn into the three Cessnas filling the left side of the hangar. Either option would end in a crash. With luck, I might escape the wreck and the building before fire consumed both. All this coursed through my mind in one or two seconds. I didn't think of shutting the engine off or jumping from the moving airplane.

I turned. My flash reasoning was that it would look better doing something other than continuing straight ahead. I shoved the left rudder pedal to the firewall. The Colt responded in a surprisingly tight turn. The airplane tipped to the right on two wheels. The tires squealed and the right wing dropped under the left wing of the nearest Cessna, but did not scrape the floor. The Colt continued around its sharp turn and out the door without hitting anything. I pushed the right rudder pedal to stop the turn and pulled the mixture control to kill the engine. The airplane glided to the other side of the ramp.

Bush pilots have an expression, "Stopping a floatplane is like trying to stop a pee midstream. It can turn your toenails black." My toenails were black.

"You should be more careful," Hector said when he reached the Colt. I was still in the pilot's seat. I knew my legs wouldn't hold me.

"We never taxi the Colt into the hangar," Hector continued. "We always shut it down and coast. The brakes don't work very well, you know. It's lucky you didn't hit anything."

I gave him a look that would have stopped a train, but Hector wasn't an eye-contact man. I thought the incident would spell the end of my one-day employment at Pie In The Sky, the end of my quick rise to chief flying instructor, and the end of my unmentioned salary. But Hector connected a towbar to the Colt's nosewheel without saying any more. I got out onto my wobbly legs and helped him push the airplane back into the hangar. We parked it over the two curved black marks the Colt's tires had left on the floor.

By the time we were done, I had decided the incident wasn't really my fault, but thought I should say something humble anyway. "I'm sorry about that little stunt, Hector. I suppose if I were you I'd have fired me by now."

The comment made him smile. He put his hand on my shoulder and said, "Well I might have, except I did the same thing myself when I started here three years ago, so I'd have to fire me too. Let's both stay and maybe this time we can talk the mechanic into tightening up the brakes."

4/ Clod Hoppers and College Students

Despite my roller coaster first day of instructing at the Pie In The Sky flying school, I was optimistic about my new job. The key was the students. Teaching flying can be enjoyable, given the right customers. They don't have to be particularly intelligent, coordinated, or talented, if they're at least borderline normal and carry a dose of motivation. The job can be fun. The Pie customers seemed to fit the bill.

The flying school manager was another story. Seeing him stunt flying the Cessna 172 with his family on board had knocked a lot out of my new-job euphoria, but even he had turned out not too badly.

On day two I was looking forward to becoming more familiar with the new airplanes and getting back into the instructing groove. The manager was off, so the only question of the day was meeting the other flying instructor. If his head was on reasonably straight, then my optimism would not be wasted.

I walked into the office and was greeted by Roger — seven-foot Roger — 250-pound Roger. Roger Daley was a small house on two legs dressed in a parka. He smiled, extended a huge hand and said, "Hi, you must be the new guy. Hector told me about you last night."

Roger was the other instructor. I couldn't imagine how he fit into Cessna 150s. I should have replied, "Yes, how do you do," but it was early in the morning and my jaw went another way.

"How do you fit into a Cessna 150?" I blurted out.

Roger laughed — a booming, big-man laugh. "It's a squeeze, that's for sure," he said. "I've always figured if I had a student my size, we'd have to get married to fly together legally." He laughed again.

I decided I might like working with Roger.

"Come on," he said, "give me a hand pulling out the airplanes."

We walked around to the old wooden hangar. The door consisted of 20 panels hung from an overhead track. Roger started at the middle and pushed half the panels at once. This was significant. The night before, Hector and I had had a hard time closing them. Over the years, the building had sagged and the ground had heaved. The two of us had had to push on each panel together to move them.

I stared while Roger shouldered 10 panels. They probably weighed 1,000 pounds each. They didn't move easily, but they did move. He did both sides on his own, not to show off, but because I was standing there with my mouth open instead of helping.

I definitely was going to enjoy working with Roger.

I assumed we would drive the aircraft out, since Hector had driven them in. Not with Roger; he pushed the Cessna 172 from behind and pulled a Cessna 150 at the same time, herding the two airplanes around to the gas pumps. I pulled the other Cessna 150 out and followed him. Roger fueled the three of them while I went back for the Colt. They were all high-wing airplanes with gas tanks on top. He didn't use the ladder.

Roger and I went back to the office where he filled me in, as best he could, on Hector's students that I was to fly with that day. The customers at Pie In The Sky were a strange mix. Half were local farmers and the rest were college students. The students came as a result of a learn-to-fly discount package that we offered to the local college. The farmers came because it was November, their payday.

The farmers were older men with grown children and paid mortgages. Learning to fly was a present to themselves, the realization of a lifelong dream of escaping the dust and mud for the sky. They approached each one-hour lesson as a half-day's entertainment, which made teaching them enjoyable. This was good because they were slow learners. Most spoke English as a second language and were a generation away from any formal schooling.

My first student that day was Orval Swick, a leather-faced tobacco farmer built like a stump. He came in looking for Hector. When he saw Ursula he smiled and spoke in a cheerful, accented voice. "Hello little girl, how are you?"

"I'm fine thank you Orval," she replied and smiled back. Motioning toward me, she said, "Orval, I'd like you to meet our new flying instructor."

Orval was already sizing me up. His friendly smile faded as he realized my presence was going to upset his routine. Orval was typical of the Pie area farmers I was to meet — curious, friendly and shy. His worried face made it obvious that Orval's cast-in-stone plans for the day didn't include having a flying lesson with a stranger.

"Pleased to meet you," he said. The handshake was firm, but the tone was cautious. "Vere is Hector?" he asked, directing the question to Ursula.

"He took a day off since we have a new pilot," Ursula said. She tried to make it sound like a good idea.

Orval frowned seriously.

I did my best to ease the situation. "I'm pleased to meet you, Orval,"

I said with a friendly smile. "Did you know your name is important in aviation history? Orval Wright was the first man to fly a heavier-than-air craft. He was a bicycle mechanic who built the first aircraft with his brother."

"Ya, I knew vas good name," Orval replied. "but Orville Vight vas second to fly. His brudder, Vilbur vas first. Orville won da coin toss to go first on day before, but he bended da ving on takeoff. It took dem whole day to fix. Den vas Vilbur turn. But like you say, Orville is good aviation name." Then he added with a laugh, "He spell it different, but maybe he change it."

Working in Pie, I eventually learned there wasn't much I could tell a farmer. What they didn't know, they weren't interested in. But the small talk broke the ice. Orval started to relax. I took him to a corner of the lounge for a pre-flight briefing. The lesson was an introduction to crosswind takeoffs and landings. I wanted to make sure he understood the concept of drift before we went flying.

"Orval, do you know when the airplane is flying crossways to the wind, it's flying straight through the air, but the air is moving across the ground making it look like the airplane is flying sideways?"

He furrowed his brow, "You say ven airplane is flying sideways, it's not. It's vind flying sideways and plane is goin' straight?"

"Ah, sort of," I said, hoping to make myself clear. "But the wind doesn't push on the side of the airplane; the airplane is suspended in an airmass that's moving sideways over the ground."

The furrows in his brow deepened. "Vell, I don't know; maybe I stupid. In old country ve say, 'Thresh into da vind and vear da chaff.' Are ve talkin' 'bout the same t'in?"

"Well, almost, but today we're going to approach the runway crossways to the wind, so I'm trying to explain sideways drift."

"Ya?"

This was going to be tough. I tried another tack. "If a man wanted to spit into a gopher hole in a gale," I explained, "he'd aim into the wind."

I watched for his reaction. There was none. He watched me for more explanation. There was none.

"Do you understand?" I asked, hopefully.

"Ya, I tink so,"

"Good. Now imagine the man is spitting into the gopher hole from a moving tractor."

"Dat vould be harder," he offered, but he still looked puzzled.

"Right. Same if we're flying toward a runway for landing. We'd aim the airplane windward to get there. We're going to practise that today."

"Okay," Orval said. It was obvious he wasn't sure about all this, but I continued anyway.

"The next thing you need to know is that we can't land like that, because the airplane would be going sideways over the ground."

"You said it vould look like it was going sidevays," he said.

"I did, but it'll look like it's going sideways through the air, when you look at the ground, but it's not."

He looked doubtful.

"Well, don't worry about that. The other thing I want you to know is about sideslipping. In order to make the airplane go straight down the runway when it's drifting, we're going to bank into the wind to make it go sideways through the air, but we have to use opposite rudder to prevent it from turning."

Orval's expression changed from doubtful to worried. "You say is not going sidevays, but now ve vant to go sidevays to go straight?"

"Right."

He didn't understand, but I decided we'd both had enough of my low-tech briefing. "Let's go flying," I said.

"Ya, good idea."

In the airplane I demonstrated the first takeoff and landing, repeating my explanations. Then I asked Orval to try it. On the approach to landing, rather than just pointing the Cessna 150 into the wind and holding it there to see the results, Orval worked the controls back and forth. I was on the receiving end of his flailing elbows.

"Orval, pretend the runway is the gopher hole and the airplane is the spit. Just take aim and hold it. We'll worry about the corrections later."

He set his jaw and aimed to the right of the runway. It worked. "Now put the airplane into a sideslip for the landing," I said.

He went back to sawing the controls. "Orval, pretend I'm a fat person sitting on the right side of the boat. That would bank the airplane to the right and you'd have to push the rudder to go straight."

That helped. After a few circuits, Orval understood the concepts. He was going to need more practise, but he had the idea. By the end of the lesson we were good friends. He booked another lesson with me, and with a laugh, promised to think about spitting into gopher holes and steering lopsided boats.

I was on a roll, so I gave the same crosswind lesson to my next student. Justin Hanover was typical of the college side of our customer mix. He was young, smart and sharp.

I introduced myself. Justin gave my hand a quick pump and said, "Hi. How long will we be?"

"It's a one-hour lesson," I replied.

"Great," he said, "Ready to go? I don't have much more than that before my next class."

"Sure, but first I want to go over some background for the lesson."

"Okay, shoot," he said, checking his watch.

"Justin, if you wanted to spit into a gopher hole in a gale from a moving tractor, do you understand that you would have to lead the hole to windward?"

He looked at me like I was drugged. "Whatever you say," he replied cautiously, "It's been a long time since I spit into a gopher hole — from a tractor, — in a gale."

"I'm talking about wind drift."

"Are you asking me about crabbing on approach for a crosswind landing?"

"Right. We're going to practise that today."

"Fine," he said and started to get up.

"Before we go, I'll outline the landing technique. I want you to imagine steering a boat with a fat person sitting on the right side."

"What aviation manoeuver are you de-identifying this time?" he asked.

"Sideslipping for crosswind landings," I replied.

"Bank the aircraft into the wind to match the drift; use opposite rudder to keep it straight. How am I doing?"

"Fine," I said.

"Good, now what's this above fat boat people?"

"Never mind. Let's go flying."

After I made the generation adjustment, Justin and I got along fine. He was impatient but easy to teach. And he flew well.

I was going to like instructing at Pie. The variety of flying with the Orvals and Justins was a good challenge. I finished the crosswind lesson with Justin and made sure he booked with me again.

"Do you want to fly on Saturday?" I asked.

"Negative, never on the weekend; that's ski time," he said. "I've got time between classes on Friday around two o'clock."

"Fine, see you then," I replied.

"In the meantime," he said with a grin, "I'll look for wet-headed gophers."

It took me a second to catch on, "Right, and watch out for fat boat people."

5/ Tidbits

When Susan and I were looking for a place to stay in Pie, our salaries said, "small apartment over store." But we weren't apartment people. We had moved from the wide-open Canadian north with a German shepherd and a horse.

Susan found an old farm house on the edge of town for rent at an apartment price. The farm land had been subdivided into housing but the developer had left the original homestead. The furniture was early Salvation Army and there wasn't anywhere to keep a horse, but it was a whole house and yard to ourselves.

The surrounding new homes were all upper middle class. The farm had been carved into large lots and sold to people who either had money or wanted everyone to think they did. The crummiest car in the neighbourhood was a three-year old Volvo. The farmhouse had been "updated" with crooked, green vinyl clapboard. With our sagging Volkswagen parked outside, it stuck out like a sore thumb.

The neighbours ignored us. We didn't mind. We were many dollars and a generation apart from most of them. We were busy with new jobs, so we ignored them back.

But our dog didn't. Lady stayed in the house when we were at work, but her nose told her the neighbours were cooking better stuff than she would get from us. When we let her out one evening that first week, an invisible vortex of roast beef fumes sucked her to the next house. She sat and drooled against the neighbour's sliding glass doors.

Our telephone rang. "Hello, this is Mrs. Cunningham. I live next door. I believe it is your German shepherd sitting on my back porch. I wonder if you would mind my giving her a leftover from our supper?"

"I'm sorry the dog is bothering you Mrs. Cunningham," I said. "I'll be right over to get her."

"Well, I don't mind her being here. She doesn't make any noise but she does look hungry. I'm sure you must feed her but I thought I could give her a little tidbit."

"That's very nice of you but I'm afraid you'd be stuck with her forever. I'll come over and bring her home."

"Oh, all right."

When I reached the Cunningham's back door, the dog gave me a "who asked you" look. A large, matronly lady in her early 60s was waiting on the other side of the glass. She slid the doors open. "Hello, I'm Mrs. Cunningham. I wrapped up at little something for the dog. Perhaps you could give it to her at home and maybe she won't be the wiser."

"That's kind of you Mrs. Cunningham. You didn't really need to. I'm embarrassed Lady is bothering you."

"Lady, that's an appropriate name," she said, "and don't be embarrassed. She is very well behaved."

I took the foil-wrapped bundle, but left her holding the silver tray. "Thank you very much."

I didn't have to coax Lady home. She knew damn well what was in the package and who it was for.

"Susan, come see this," I said, when I opened the foil. The "tidbit" was most of a two-kilogram roast. The Cunninghams had taken the two outside slices and left the rest. We carved the roast for supper and made sandwiches with the leftovers.

"If this dog is going to bite anyone in her life," Susan said, "It's going to be us, right now."

She didn't, but she drooled on the kitchen floor until we gave her the nude bone.

The next day Mrs. Cunningham was greeted by Lady's dog-smile pressed against the glass. They became good friends. Dr. Cunningham was a surgeon who worked long hours. So did we. Lady and Mrs. Cunningham kept each other company during the day. The dog grew fat on scones and jam, liver paté, and roast beef. We stopped buying dog kibble because she wouldn't touch it. She condescended to sleep with us because she couldn't eat anymore. We went to bed serenaded by the belches and rumbles of rich food being digested in a happy dog.

6/ Day of Reckoning

"I've been watching you with the students," Hector said. He was helping Roger and me pull out the airplanes. "You're doing a good job," he continued, "but I have a few suggestions."

I was surprised. I had been busy flying with Hector's students for five days and rarely saw him. When Hector came to work, he pulled out the airplanes and then disappeared until the end of the day. He was chatty and friendly when he was around, but mostly he was out of sight and out of mind.

There had been no more incidents of illegal aerobatics to make me wish I hadn't taken the Pie job. This was the first time since I'd been hired that Hector had said anything to indicate his role as manager. Roger stood behind him looking happy that I was the target of the "suggestions".

"I noticed you do ground briefings with each student," he said. "A little talk doesn't hurt, but students learn better by doing. Don't waste time on the ground when you could be up there giving the customers practical experience."

I guessed he was referring to the fact that flying hours were revenue and briefing was not. His comments had nothing to do with teaching technique, but I went along as if they had.

"I understand, Hector," I said, "but someone like Orval Swick needs a briefing to make sure he is on track."

"That's okay, but don't cut into the flying time so much."

"Okay, Hector," I replied, making a mental note to forget what he said.

"And another thing," Hector continued, "I noticed you're doing a walkaround inspection with the students on every flight. That's another waste of flying time. It's okay to show them the preflight, but not every time. That's why we check the aircraft in the morning, so the students don't have to."

Skipping the preflight inspection was new to me. I didn't let it go by. "How are the students going to develop good habits," I offered, "if they don't practise things like the walkaround? I thought you said students learn by doing?"

"I did, but that's in the air, not on the ground. Just show them how to do it a couple of times and that's enough. Students learn best by example. If you let them do the walkaround, they'll leave the gas caps off or something. If the airplanes get checked every flight, we'll wear them out. Things like the oil access door will need replacing all the time."

I could think of several arguments against what Hector was saying, but I decided it wouldn't be worth it.

"Whatever you say Hector."

"Just to show you, I'll fly with Gloria Simcoe this morning," he said.

Hector's comments irked me. I suppose it was his sudden managerial spirit that got under my skin. He appeared to do no work and was rarely around. It was hard to imagine how he qualified to be my boss.

Gloria Simcoe was the first student on the day's booking sheet. It would be Hector's first lesson since I'd started at Pie In The Sky. Roger was grinning.

"But first I'm going to do a weather check," Hector added.

There was no weather office or flight service station at Pie. If the conditions were marginal, we had to fly a circuit to see if it was good enough to fly.

I left Hector at the gas pumps and went back to the office. There was a good looking university coed waiting inside.

Ursula introduced us, "This is Gloria Simcoe."

"Hi Gloria, pleased to meet you," I said. "Hector will fly with you this morning. He's doing a weather check first. He shouldn't be long. Are you from the university?"

It was a dumb, small-talk question. Beautiful 19-year old blondes didn't farm.

"Yes," she replied politely, "how did you know?"

"Lucky guess."

We both watched Hector climb into the Cessna 150 and take off. He did no warmup or pre-takeoff check, and he didn't use the runway. He just started the airplane and took off straight from the pumps, down the taxiway and into the air.

I was as surprised as Gloria, but she spoke first. "Is he supposed to do that?"

"Oh sure," I said. The incident had spiked my uncertainty about working under Hector. It also activated the evil side of my brain. "We depart the ramp all the time. We just make sure it's into the wind and there's no traffic. Have you never done it?"

"No, Hector never mentioned it."

"Well today is a good time to start. Hector will have run the airplane so it will be warm and you'll know everything is working fine. If the weather is a go, skip your checks and blast off from the ramp."

"Okay, sounds like fun," she said.

As if to put his stamp of approval on the idea, Hector landed — on the ramp.

He strutted into the office like a peacock. "Good morning Gloria," he said in a silly musical voice. "The ceiling is high enough for circuits. We can practise those landings of yours. Ready to go?"

"Yes."

"Good. No sense wasting time on the ground," he added, looking my way. "I'm ready when you are."

I followed them out the door to help Roger fuel the rest of the fleet.

"Watch this," I said to Roger, motioning toward Hector and Gloria. They were already climbing into the airplane.

"Watch what?"

"You'll see."

"All I see is our lecherous leader helping Gloria with her seat belt," he said.

"Watch them after she gets the airplane started."

"Okay."

It was perfect. Once the seat belts were on, Hector relaxed. Gloria started the Cessna, looked both ways and moved forward a little to line up with the taxiway. Then she shoved the throttle to the firewall.

It took Hector six beats to realize what was happening. Another three beats went by while he uncrossed his legs and got them on the rudder/brake pedals. By then the aircraft was accelerating through 50 mph and Gloria was pulling back on the elevator control.

The airplane pitched forward as Hector slammed on the brakes. The main wheels locked and the Cessna's tires painted two black lines down the taxiway with the engine still at full power. Eventually he got her hand off the throttle and the airplane wiggled to a stop.

There was a long period while they sat there. The airplane was rocking a little from Hector's gestures. He looked back at me. Even from that distance I could tell he wasn't smiling.

"Did you set her up?" Roger asked.

"Yup," I replied. I still didn't know Roger or Hector very well. I wasn't sure how they would react to my little stunt, but it was too late now. "I gave her a 'monkey see, monkey do' pep talk in the office while Hector was flying his weather check."

"You're a bugger," he said with a laugh.

"Thank you," I replied.

"Just be careful with Hector. He has a sense of humour, but occasionally he remembers to be the manager. You can push him too far."

"Okay, thanks for the advice."

Hector and Gloria turned the airplane around and taxied slowly to the runway for another takeoff.

I didn't have a student so I was sitting in the office when they returned from the lesson an hour later.

Hector tried to sound authoritative. "Ursula can book your next lesson," he said to Gloria. "We'll do more circuits, taking off from the runway."

"Okay Hector," Gloria replied. I think she was fighting back a smirk.

He motioned me to join him in the back office. He closed the door.

"Gloria said you told her to take off from the ramp. What do you think you were doing?"

"She saw you do it, so I told her it was okay," I replied.

"Well you know it's not," he fumed. "I'm a professional pilot with lots of experience. She's not. She might try that solo and kill someone."

He may have been right about Gloria trying it on her own, but he was exaggerating the kill rate. The taxiway was as long as the runway, and the airport was never busy. "I put her up to it to illustrate that students might try anything they see us do. If you hot dog around a flying school, it's going to happen." My argument didn't come out as strong as it was in my mind.

"If we tell them not to, they won't," Hector said. His reply also sounded a little weak.

"Did you tell Gloria not to put six people in a Cessna 172?" I asked.

"No, she knows better than to do something like that."

"Did you tell her not to do touch and goes on Highway 401?"

"No, she wouldn't do that, either."

"Chase boats on Lake Erie?"

"No, of course not."

"How about aerobatics?"

"No, she has no reason to think those are good ideas unless you tell her, like taking off from the taxiway."

"I disagree. I think students are influenced by what they see. After watching you and the folks upside down, I bet Phil Paterson can hardly wait to get a licence and take his friends for an aerobatic ride."

This wasn't working out very well. We were both getting a little frustrated.

"Look," Hector said with a sigh, "maybe we do things a little differently than where you're from, but we haven't had any problems. It's my job to make sure the school is running well. This morning I made a couple of small suggestions. If you don't like what we do, you should be talking to me, not the customers."

He was right about using the customers to make a point. I had gone too far. It was time to salvage my job.

"Hector, you're right. I shouldn't have told Gloria to depart from the ramp. I'm sorry. But I think we should set a good example in front of the students."

"Fine," he said, "we'll do that. But you're going to find lots of pilots land and take off from the taxiway here. This is not a big city airport."

"Okay, thanks for the warning. I'll look both ways before crossing the ramp."

"Good idea," he said. The suggestion made him smile a little. "And don't forget to check the sky before venturing onto Highway 401," he added.

"Okay," I said, smiling back. "what about boating?"

That made him grin even more. "Yeah, and don't forget boating. If we ever see you on the lake, Mom and I will buzz you for sure."

7/ Oops

There was a farmer talking to Ursula when I walked into the office. I knew he wasn't a college student because they didn't wear green work clothes and rubber boots.

Ursula gave me an expectant look, so I walked over.

"This is John Torrance," she said.

"Pleased to meet you," I said, accepting the lean man's gentle handshake.

I missed all the clues. The name should have registered. Ursula's extra attentiveness should have tipped me off. At least I should have noticed that the old cap read, "Pie In The Sky," but I didn't.

"Are you learning to fly, John?" I asked.

"No," he said smiling, "I have a pilot licence."

"Great," I replied, "A rental customer."

"You might say that," he said.

John Torrance owned Pie In The Sky. Ursula was literally dancing behind the counter, but she was afraid to say anything.

"Are you going up today, John?" I continued.

"No", he replied, "I just dropped by to see how it's going."

"Well, it's a nice day for flying out there," I said, walking behind the desk to check a student's file.

Hector came in. "Hello Mr. Torrance. How are you today?"

"Fine, Hector, fine, thank you," the farmer said quietly.

"Did you met our new instructor?" Hector asked.

"Yes, we were just talking about the nice flying weather," John said.

"Yeah, we're going to be busy real soon. We have students on their way." Hector seemed a little nervous. "Ursula, show Mr. Torrance the booking sheets."

Ursula turned the sheets around so the customer could see them.

"But we have openings John," I said, trying to be helpful. If you'd like to rent an airplane, I'll sign you out."

Hector looked horrified. "Mr. Torrance doesn't have to rent an airplane," he said. "He can take any one he wants, anytime, and he doesn't need you to sign him out."

That did it. I finally realized the man's importance.

"Sorry Mr. Torrance," I said sheepishly, "your name didn't click."

"That's quite all right," Torrance said, "and the name's John. I might take you up on your flying suggestion, but first I'd like to have a coffee with you, if you have time."

"Certainly sir," I said.

"John," he corrected.

"John," I replied. "My next student comes in 20 minutes."

"Fine, I'll buy."

We took our coffees into the back office. John closed the door. The talk was friendly. He asked me about myself and told me a little about Pie In The Sky.

The Torrance family owned the land next to the airport. John grew up during the war and spent hours watching air force training planes boring holes in the sky. After the war he learned to fly with the local crop duster, paying for the lessons from farm earnings. It took him three years to get a licence. Later he took over the farm from his dad and later still, bought the air service.

"The ag flying is the most profitable," he said. "The flying school/aircraft rental part of the business provides a service to the area and gives the ag pilots a job in the winter," John explained. "But Hector is a little wild and terrible when it comes to paperwork, so I'm glad he hired you. Hector's good at turning a small profit, but he needs a hand with the adminstration end of things. Perhaps you can help."

"The flying school is profitable?" I blurted out. It was my belief that small-town flying schools had to be extremely well run just to break even. I had assumed that the Hector-run part of Pie In The Sky was a money loser. I thought it survived on the profits from the agricultural flying.

"Yes, Hector has done well," John said. "In his three years as manager, we have been able to buy a new aircraft each year, mostly from the flying school profits. You sound surprised."

"Well, I guess I haven't been here long enough to notice the profitability," I said. I was back pedalling. I changed the subject. "I'll try and do my best for you as chief flying instructor."

"Good. I think I can count on you. Welcome aboard," he said, getting up from his chair. "Now I think I'll take you up on your suggestion and go flying."

8/ Hector's Folly

Hector posted a notice in the lounge about the airport being closed the following Saturday for a bicycle rodeo. I couldn't believe it. Airports are closed for airshows, bad weather or construction, but this was a kid's bicycle rodeo.

"Hector, are we going to lose a day's instructing and rental for this bike rodeo?"

"Yes, you'll be flying passenger hops," he said grinning like it was a good idea.

"What passenger hops?" I asked.

"On Saturday, you'll give passenger rides during the rodeo. We'll close runway 24 and 33 for the bikes, and keep runway 27 open for you and anyone else who needs to land. Roger'll answer questions and give out buttons at the Learn-to-Fly booth, Ursula will sell tickets for sightseeing flights, and you can fly them in the 172."

"You're serious, aren't you."

"Sure. My kids are in it and I'm a judge," he said with a proud smile.

If someone had asked me about trading a regular flying school day, when all four airplanes would be flying, for sightseeing flights in the 172, I would have said it was a poor management decision. I couldn't understand how Hector had made the profits to buy new airplanes while making bone-head arrangements like this.

The airport bicycle rodeo was one of the things that made Pie different. The town owned the airport, so they could do whatever they wanted with it. The Canadian government had built Pie field during the war, but had neglected it ever since. The town fathers got tired of begging for improvements and, a couple of years before I arrived, had convinced the federal government to sell them the airport for a dollar.

There were no airline flights into Pie. It was mainly a recreation airport where people could learn to fly and rent airplanes. The town placed it under the direction of the Pie Department of Parks and Recreation. When the local fall fair organizers were looking for a large piece of blacktop for a bicycle rodeo, there was no hesitation. They closed two runways for the day and used them.

I thought it was a waste of a good flying day, but I was raised in a big city. I was ignorant of the significance of fall fair time in a small town. The interruption didn't really bother the flying school customers, because the college students rarely booked lessons on their weekends and the farmer customers were helping with the bicycle rodeo or some other fair activity. It turned into a good opportunity for the Pie In The Sky staff to promote the airport to the local people who came out only on rodeo day.

When I arrived at eight o'clock on Saturday morning, the Pie police were already placing orange cones on the closed runways. Soon cars, pickup trucks and vans loaded with parents, kids and their bicycles started pulling into the parking lot. The local lunch catering trucks set up in the infield to dispense hot coffee and cold donuts.

Runways 24 and 33 were on the other side of runway 27. The problem of how several hundred bicyclists, judges and onlookers would cross an active runway was solved by school crossing guards. Two guards at each end of runway 27 proudly held up their STOP signs to the rodeo traffic while looking in all directions for airplanes. When there was a four-way agreement on the all-clear, they waved the people across.

The weather was good for mid-November in Southern Ontario. There was a nip in the air, but the wind was light and the sun was warming things up.

Ursula and Roger arrived and carried a pair of tables from the ground school classroom in the basement of the terminal building to the outside to use as a booth. They set up a bristol board sign made by Hector.

Sightseeing Flights - $3 each

It was too cheap. At the time we were charging $28 an hour for the Cessna 172 with a pilot. A normal sightseeing flight was 20 to 25 minutes plus loading and unloading. Averaging two flights an hour at Hector's rates, we would lose $10 an hour.

"Ursula, does Hector's sign mean $9 a load?" I asked.

"That's right," she said. "He said to do five-minute flights. With a five-minute turnaround, we'll make an extra $26 an hour."

The man was dumb. I knew there was no way we could squeeze six flights into an hour, but Hector was on the other side of the field. I decided to say nothing and show him it wouldn't work.

By the time I had the 172 out and gassed, a father and his two boys

31

were waiting for me at the edge of the ramp with their $3 tickets. The kids were as excited as popcorn on a hot stove. The looks on their wide-eyed faces made me forget about Hector's folly.

When we taxied out to the runway, there was a flurry of STOP sign waving by the crossing guards. They held up the stream of people, bikes and strollers, so we could take off.

I pulled onto the runway and applied full power. The roar of the engine cut into the happy squeals coming from the back seat. When we were airborne, I stole a quick look at the boys. Their faces were pressed against the side windows watching the shrinking picture of activity below.

I flew over the town of Pie so the dad could find their house and point it out to the boys. Above the engine noise I could hear typical first time passenger comments such as, "the cars are like toys", and "the people look like ants". I didn't worry about Hector's five-minute limit because I knew there wouldn't be many customers that early.

I landed 20 minutes later to find six people lined up on the edge of the ramp. I cut the next two flights a little shorter, but still flew over Pie. There weren't any other points of interest near the airport except the bicycle rodeo. Each time I landed there were more people waiting than the time before. On the third flight I had the time down to 12 minutes plus turnaround.

I was falling behind. The lineup continued to grow. I was right; $3 was cheap and the town was taking advantage of it. By the end of the first hour, there were about 20 people waiting. I trimmed time off each flight until I was flying just a big circuit around the airport. The bicycle rodeo was the only thing the passengers saw, but no one complained. By the end of the second hour I hit Hector's planned time limit of five and five, but the line kept growing. The airplane needed fuel and I needed the washroom.

Roger came to the rescue. He approached my side of the airplane between flights. "When you need gas, park by the pumps. I'll fill it while you take a break."

"Okay, after this one."

Some break — it didn't take Roger long to refuel the airplane. He was done when I came out of the washroom and the lineup was snowballing. The large group attracted attention. People who normally wouldn't pay anything for an airplane ride bought tickets because everyone else did.

I flew tight circuits and got the time down to four minutes. It didn't dent the size of the waiting crowd, but it kept the crossing guards busy.

As soon as the pedestrian traffic filled in behind my takeoff, I would be swinging around for a landing. Each approach was preceded by a flurry of STOP sign waving to clear the runway. After a while the guards caught on to how many people they could start across before I would swoop back for a landing.

Initially, I thought the short flights would appear chintzy on our part. As my boredom factor increased, I didn't think that anymore. Four minutes was almost too long for some of the kids whose stomachs had had too much junk food and too much excitement. I didn't lose any but a few were close.

The day passed in a slow blur. Roger gassed the airplane for me every two hours and Ursula occasionally passed me a coffee and stale donut. I didn't mind that Roger didn't offer to fly. I knew it took him five minutes just to get in the plane. With him in the pilot's seat, the rear seat passengers wouldn't have seen anything.

I never did catch up. Toward the end of the afternoon, Roger pulled out a Cessna 150 and flew the kids who had won the various rodeo classes, as promised, one at a time. The people waiting for me started to think more about supper and less about a sightseeing flight. The crowd thinned out on its own. I had no idea how many times I flew, but it was more than enough. I didn't need another passenger hop for a long time.

"Sixty-seven flights," Ursula said when I staggered into the office. Hector was there. It was dark. "One hundred and seventy-seven passengers not counting Roger's freebees; $531."

We had doubled the aircraft's normal 10-hour income. I was too dizzy and tired to care. "Well, I don't need to fly another one of those for a long time," I said.

Hector smirked, "I hope tomorrow is soon enough. I told Ursula to rebook all the people who couldn't wait today. There are 37 of them coming tomorrow. It's my day off and Roger has students."

9/ Honk

Roger went duck hunting with the Cessna 172 on Thursday and didn't come back. He phoned from a french fry stand on the Long Point beach.

"Hi. I had a little problem," he told Ursula. "I'm okay, but I'll need Wilbur, some furnace vent pipe and lots of tape before I can fly out of here. And you'd better call Soil and Sea to come and get Mel."

The "little problem" was a five-kilogram Canada goose through the windshield. Roger had been flying on a bird count for the Department of Soil & Sea. The marshy deltas along the north shore of Lake Erie were spring and fall rest stops for migratory birds. The DSS felt obliged to count them. The idea was to regulate the length of the hunting season to reflect any shift in the number of birds.

For four days, Roger flew along the coast with Mel Armstrong, the DSS observer in the right seat counting the flocks in the air.

"Forty Canadas, twenty-five Mergansers, thirteen Mallards…," Mel would count into a tape recorder.

On Thursday, they found a large flock of Canada geese. Mel counted while Roger circled the formation, intent on not running into them. He didn't see the other flock. He flew right into another V of Canadas. Several birds bounced off the plane and one took out Roger's side of the Cessna's plastic windshield, but not before being chewed by the prop. The result was that Roger was hit square in the face by pieces of windshield, an eighty-mph blast of cold air, and the gory remains of the goose. He wasn't badly hurt, but neither he nor Mel knew that.

The bird hit the plane with a bang. Mel looked at Roger and all he saw was his pilot clawing at a gory mess where his face had been. First Mel swore and then he realized he was going to die. He screamed.

Roger was clawing at his face because he couldn't breathe or see. He realized the windshield was gone, so he throttled back and raised the nose on the aircraft to slow down. He wiped his face some more and managed to clear one watery eye. Roger didn't know how badly he or the airplane was damaged so he started a descent for the beach. He leaned toward Mel to escape some of the wind that was freezing the goose gore to his face. Poor Mel thought he was slumping over in the last throes of dying. He could see they were headed for the ground. He screamed louder.

Roger's one-eyed approach was good enough and the beach was clear. With what Mel thought was a death plunge, he sideslipped the airplane down to a landing without further damage.

"I was relieved to get stopped," Roger told us afterward. "It got rid of the wind in my face, but when I shut the engine down, the noise continued. It was Mel still screaming. His eyes were closed and he was still waiting for the impact."

When Mel finally realized they had made it, the screams turned to sobs. He was badly shaken. Roger washed his face in the lake. He had suffered a few minor cuts, but the cold air had already stopped the bleeding. He hiked down the beach and called Pie In The Sky.

I drove out to the beach in the pickup truck with Hector and Wilbur Olmstead, the air service's old mechanic.

The Cessna was damaged in several places. Bird strikes had opened the thin aluminum in two places on the leading edge of the wing and one on the tail. Half of the one-piece windshield was gone. There was blood everywhere.

Mel was also wrecked - emotionally. He had stopped crying, but he was obviously upset. A DSS truck took him away shortly after we arrived.

It was obvious that Wilbur was an experienced crop dusting mechanic familiar with repairing damage in the field from bird and wire strikes. In twenty minutes he had taped pieces of soft aluminum furnace pipe over the holes, including the windshield.

Hector declared that he would fly the airplane back using the dual controls in the right seat. He checked out the beach while Wilbur finished the repairs. "There, that should hold if he don't get caught in the rain," Wilbur chuckled.

He didn't.

That would be the end of the story except for a secretary at the Soil and Sea office who used a Dictaphone to type out the bird count from the tape recording. She heard the whole thing. "Thirty Mergansers, twenty-seven Canadas, fifty-seven Mallards. BANG! WHAT THE —; AHHHHHHHHHHHHHHHHHHHHHHHHHHHHHHHHHHHHHHHHH."

The scream lasted over four minutes. Mel had left the microphone open all the way down.

10/ The Hangar Club

On a bad weather day in late November, I joined the Pie In The Sky
"Hangar Club." This was the unofficial group that collected in
Wilbur's shop daily. Every airport has them. The common bond was
talk. The members watched Wilbur work and told flying stories that got
longer and more exaggerated with each recounting. It was a close-knit,
friendly bunch. Strangers with fresh ears were welcome, as long as they
didn't monopolize the conversation.

When I arrived at work that rainy morning, low cloud made it obvious there would be no flying. Hector was already in the office. It was
Roger's day off.

"Good morning, looks like the ducks'll be walking today," he said
with a grin.

"I think you're right."

"Come on out to the hangar and we'll have some of Wilbur's coffee."

Wilbur's office, shop and storeroom were built along the side of the
old hangar. He was already there stoking a rusty Quebec stove.

"Coffee ready, Wilbur?" Hector asked.

"Just about."

Wilbur was a lean, older man with bent posture and a wrinkled
face. His grubby coveralls were a crusty record of years of aircraft
maintenace.

"Help yourself," Hector said, pointing to a few mugs on a table. He
wiped one out with his finger and filled it from an enamel pot that had
been sitting on the stove.

I followed his lead, picking the least offensive cup. The "coffee" was
thick and black. Its surface had that iridescence of gasoline floating on
water. It didn't smell like coffee.

"Coffee, cod liver oil and rum," Hector volunteered. "Wilbur was
weaned on it down east. Have a seat," He motioned to several old tube
and plywood chairs that looked like refugees from a collapsed
auditorium.

I took one sip and regretted it for the rest of the day. But I didn't say
anything. I hadn't spent much time with Wilbur, so I vowed to be

friendly and get to know our mechanic a little better. I sat and warmed my hands on the cup while Wilbur and Hector talked about the work they were doing to repair the Cessna 172.

From their conversation I gathered that Hector preferred helping Wilbur to flying with student pilots, although the definition of "helping" included more talk than work. I also learned that Hector spent significant time sitting in the big torpedo bombers parked in the back of the hangar and daydreaming about flying one during the upcoming spray season.

Over the next hour, two regular members of the Hangar Club joined us. Leon Welsh and Frank Kurzac were both Pie In The Sky spray pilots. They worked on contracts for the spring and early summer, but unlike Hector and Roger, they preferred to scrape through the rest of the year on unemployment insurance rather than teach flying. As Frank explained to me, "I'd rather starve than die at the hands of some pea-brained, motor moron, kamikaze student."

Frank was the skinnier of the two and did most of the talking. "Leon and I got well and truly bagged last night," Frank said. Leon grinned an acknowledgement. "At one point I thought I could jump out the window and fly home," Leon continued, laughing at his own joke. "Say, Leon, why didn't you try and stop me?"

"Hell, I thought you could make it," Leon said with a snort.

I listened to the slow conversation for most of the morning, nursing the coffee without actually drinking it. Whenever the pot got low, Wilbur added more rum.

The general shop scenario was Wilbur working, Hector helping, and Leon, Frank, and anyone else who dropped by, commenting. Wilbur had removed the damaged sections of the Cessna and was in the process of repairing them. He deliberated over each piece, receiving no end of advice about the relative merits of fixing versus replacing. The discussion bounced from the marital status of the parents of the Cessna engineers who designed the aircraft, to world events, and back.

Hector held one of the bent ribs from the wing's leading edge while Wilbur contemplated straightening it.

"That rib's history," Frank said, knowing Wilbur rarely bought replacement parts. "You bend that back and it'll crack for sure."

Wilbur just smiled, rearranging the wrinkles on his face.

"I kinda liked the taped-on furnace pipe," Leon offered.

"Yeah, but would it stand up to Hector's flying?" Frank asked with a chuckle.

"Hell, he's got long arms," Leon said. "He could fly and retape at the same time."

I enjoyed seeing the comraderie, but couldn't help thinking that Hector was wasting his time and John Torrance's money. It was hard to believe the flying school was profitable after watching the manager loafing in the hangar. I wondered how well Pie In The Sky would do with everyone pulling his weight.

Two other hangers-on dropped by during the morning. Both were local private pilots with aircraft based at the airport. Richard McCabe was an appliance repair man who owned a Fleet Canuck. He often took time between house calls to stop by and add his comments to the shop.

Dagmire Wilson was a barn painting salesman. Judging by the size of his new car, he was successful at it, but he had a reputation for being cheap. Dag owned an early model Cessna 150. I had not seen it move as long as I had been there.

I had met all these men before. I hadn't been at Pie In The Sky very long before they individually came into the flying school office to chat up Ursula and check out the new instructor. This was the first time I had spent any time with them on their territory.

"So you flew in the bush, eh?" Richard said. It was more of a statement than a question. "I bet you had some tight ones."

I took that as my cue to tell my best hairy bush story, but before I could say anything, Frank continued. "I flew up north once, boy, never again. I got lost for sure. There's lots to see. The only problem is, it's the same damn tree repeated several trillion times."

They all laughed and then took turns relating forgotten bush flying tales. I never did get to contribute to the conversation. After an appropriately friendly length of time, I took my leave and went back to the flying school office to prepare a ground school lesson and nurse my raging stomach.

11/ Passenger X

The week after Roger's goose encounter, he was booked on a charter flight.

"What's this trip to Sault Ste. Marie?" he asked. Roger and I had arrived the same time that morning. He had been off the day before.

"I don't know. Hector must have booked it last night," I said. It was the first I had heard of the trip.

Normally a flight away from the confines of the student practice area was a treat for us, but the Cessna 172 was still being repaired. Roger would have to fly the 500 kilometres, each way, in a Cessna 150. Watching him fit into the two-seat airplanes reminded me of trying to stuff a jack-in-the-box back into the box. The cabin of the Cessna 150 was slightly smaller than the front half of my Volkswagen Beetle and only marginally faster. After a three-hour flight, it wasn't likely Roger would spring out.

On the booking sheet, the slot for student's or passenger's name simply read, "X." It was Hector's handwriting. It was his day off.

"Do you want me to take it?" I volunteered.

"No, your students have had enough instructor changes already," Roger said. "I'll do it. Maybe the passenger won't mind if we stop half way for a stretch." Roger checked the clock. "Mr. X should be here soon according to this. Let's pull the airplanes out."

Mr. X arrived on time — in an ambulance. We found out that he was a she, and that she was dead. Roger's "passenger" was a corpse. "Mrs. X" had been a chronic patient at the Pie Provincial Hospital and had died the day before. Her family lived in Sault Ste. Marie. The funeral home had arranged for the body to be flown there for burial.

Lake Huron in the Great Lakes chain made the drive from Sault Ste. Marie a two-day round trip in a hearse, so the funeral home had called Pie In The Sky for a charter flight. Hector had taken the call. It was a revenue flight and Roger was available. That's all Hector needed to say "yes." It didn't matter to him that the only aircraft flyable were two-seaters.

The ambulance backed up to the hangar where Roger and I were pulling out the airplanes. When the attendants opened the rear doors to reveal a black body bag, Roger's changes in expression were classic. The look on his face went from confusion to disbelief to homicidal. He was normally an even-tempered guy, but if Hector had been there, they would have needed another body bag.

There was no way I was going to offer to take the flight now. "The good news is, your passenger won't mind if you stop along the way," I said with a stupid grin splitting my face. I couldn't help it.

"I don't believe this," Roger said, shaking his head.

The ambulance attendants peered into the hangar past the three airplanes we had pulled out. They were looking for something bigger.

"Where's your airplane?" one of them asked.

"Right here," Roger said, pointing to the nearest Cessna 150.

"You're kidding," the attendant said.

"Someone is kidding, but it isn't me," Roger replied. Then he added, "They won't be laughing when I get back."

Roger asked them to wait while he fetched some tools to remove the right seat. He came back with Wilbur. As soon as the old mechanic saw what was happening, he rattled off one-liners as fast as he could make them up. "Well, I'll be darned. Looks like Hector really 'stiffed' you on this one. Are you going to 'dead reckon' your way to the Soo? You know, we should really be loading the body through the 'terminal' building. Well, if you crash, we'll know there'll be at least one fatality."

Loading the body proved to be difficult. Wilbur removed the right hand door and the ambulance attendants bent Mrs. X in half. After much swearing, we shoe-horned her in and laid her out on the floor beside the pilot's seat.

Roger signed for his "cargo" and departed as soon as he fuelled the airplane. He was gone all day.

The weather was bad the next morning. Hector and I were in the shop checking the progress on the Cessna 172 when Roger came in. Frank and Leon were also there.

"Roger, how ya doin'," Frank said with a smile. "I hear you had a date with Mrs. X yesterday. Did you get lucky?"

"She would've turned you down, Frank" Roger said with a smile. "It was an interesting flight."

"What happened?" Frank asked. Hector kept quiet in the background.

"The first leg was no problem," Roger explained, pouring himself some of Wilbur's breakfast mix. "Of course, there was a headwind. I stopped in Wiarton for fuel and a stretch. The lineboy looked at the bodybag long and hard, but he didn't ask what it was and I didn't tell him."

"On the next leg I went for altitude so I could island hop across the lake within gliding distance to the shore. Passing through 5,000 feet, I thought I could hear gurgling noises coming from the heater, but then I realized that airplane heaters don't gurgle." Roger paused and sipped his coffee. He had our attention and he milked it well.

"Do you know how the lack of pressure at altitude gives you gas?" he asked. We all knew and we could guess what he was going to say next. "From the sound and smell, she must have had it coming out both ends. As soon as I got near Manitoulin, I descended again, but she must have messed herself, because the smell never went away." He paused again and sipped more coffee. "I opened the vents for some air, but it didn't help."

"That would've been it for me," Frank said. "I would've jumped, parachute or not. I don't know how you did it."

"Well I don't think I'll have to do it again. The funeral home wasn't too happy."

Hector finally spoke up. "Why do you say that? What happened?"

"The whole family came out to the airport to see granny come home. They were all waiting on the ramp when I taxied in. They were a little upset because I was an hour late but that wasn't the half of it. The old girl must have objected to the cold, because approaching the Soo, she started to sit up. That rigormortis must have set in."

Roger had been slumping in his chair. Now he slowly leaned forward, imitating the corpse. "It was weird. I could see this movement beside me. I expected the zipper to slide down and the body to pop right out. By the time I landed, she was sitting right up, pleased as punch. The family saw their deceased beloved arrive riding as a copilot in a two-seat trainer. Like I said, I don't think we'll get another call from that funeral home."

12/ The Travelling Bob and Tom Show

Acorporate turboprop aircraft regularly visited Pie. The twin-engined Beech King Air belonged to the American parent of a small bearing factory in town, one of Pie's few industries. The pilots were a pair of roly-poly, laugh-a-minute types. Bob and Tom added entertainment to our day. Everyone at the flying school looked forward to the King Air coming, except Hector. He was usually the brunt of their jokes.

"Hey Hector, what do flying school managers use for birth control?" Bob asked one day while waiting for his passengers to come back from town.

"I don't know," Hector said. He usually fell for their jokes, because he had to hear the punchline.

"Their personalities, ha, ha, ha."

One morning Hector and I were in the office when Bob and Tom dropped off passengers and didn't stay. Their home base was in Ohio, just across Lake Erie. Bob came into the lounge to make sure his passengers got a cab while Tom kept one engine running in the King Air.

"Hi there, we're heading right out again," Bob said, "We're going back home to take some passengers down state, but we'll be back this afternoon. Say Hector, why do pink flamingos stand on one leg?"

"I don't know," Hector replied.

"Because if they lifted it, they'd fall over. Ha, ha, ha. See ya later."

The airplane taxied out again. Tom announced their departure on the airport advisory frequency assigned to small, uncontrolled airports such as Pie, and they took off.

The King Air was just airborne when Tom called on the radio again. We could hear him on the monitor in the office. "Ursula, is Hector still there?"

"Affirmative," she replied.

"Ask him to come to the microphone."

"Okay, standby."

Hector had been listening and went right over to the radio. Using the microphone always made him feel important. "This is Hector, go ahead."

"Say Hector, we seem to have a slight landing gear problem. Our condition lights show an incomplete retraction. Would you do us a favour and go outside while we fly over? Maybe you'll be able to see if the wheels are all the way up?"

"Yeah, sure, right away," Hector replied and headed outside.

"Thanks, buddy, we're coming around," Tom replied.

We all watched while Hector took a position in the middle of the ramp by the office. I could see the King Air swinging around about two miles away. It started toward Hector, losing altitude and gaining speed on the way. It soon became obvious that we were in for a royal beat up. Pilots looking for a visual gear check don't normally approach the airport passing through 200 mph.

As the airplane crossed the airport boundary heading for the ramp, it was alreay down to 100 feet. I looked at Hector. He was standing out there, intent on eyeballing the landing gear. The King Air dropped to 50 feet. It was still accelerating.

At one quarter mile back the airplane was at 25 feet and going like hell. Hector hunched over a bit to make sure he could see under the plane. It dropped lower. Hector hunched down further.

When Bob and Tom approached the flying school manager, they were about fifteen feet above the ramp and doing at least 250 mph. Hector was in a full squat. It was either that or be flattened, but he never lost sight of his mission. As they zoomed over him, he snapped his head back so hard I though it was going to come off. The sudden movement sent him sprawling on his back.

But as soon as he hit the ground he was up again and running. He sprinted for the office and went straight to the radio.

"Tom," he said a little breathlessly, "the gear looks up and locked all right to me."

"Okay Hector, hee, hee; thanks a lot. See ya later, hee, hee."

"You're welcome."

Hector looked pleased with himself, like he had done something worthwhile. He still didn't get it. I was beside myself trying not to burst out laughing in his face.

"What's the matter?" Hector asked.

"I hate to tell you Hector," I said with a huge grin, "but I think they got you again."

The manager frowned. "Ursula, I'll be in the hangar if you need me," he said, and walked out.

Hector came back to the office later in the afternoon and hung around until the King Air returned. Tom called 10 miles out and asked

Ursula which runway was active.

"Say Ursula, is Hector there?" he added.

"Affirmative," she replied.

"Put him on."

"This is Hector, go ahead."

"Hector, we still seem to be having a problem with this gear. Now the lights show that it's not all the way down. Do you think you could check it for us if we fly over?"

"Sure thing; I'll be right out."

I couldn't believe he would fall for it again.

This time the King Air approached at a slower speed, but it seemed even lower with its landing gear down. I thought they really would hit him this time. Hector stood his ground, but he was almost lying down to do it. When the airplane passed over him, he didn't bother tracking it, he just kept his head down. Then he trotted into the office and to the radio.

"Yeah, I see what you mean, Tom. It looks like the left main is hung up a bit, over."

I looked at Hector in surprise. He was grinning. There was a long silence at the other end of the microphone before Tom finally spoke. "You say you saw a problem?"

"Well, it was hard to tell with you being so low, but I'm sure the left main gear was not all the way down and locked. Do you want me to call out the fire trucks from town or are you going to fly home and crash it there?" He was doing a good job of keeping the grin out of his voice.

"Ah, we got three green lights, ah, now," Tom said. "Do you suppose you could go back out with the binoculars? We'll cycle the gear and fly over again, higher up."

"Okay, I'll be right out."

The turboprop approached the ramp at a respectable 200 feet and slower than I thought a King Air could go and still stay in the air. But Hector didn't train the binoculars on it. Instead, he stood in the middle of the ramp with his arm in the air and the middle finger of that hand sticking straight up.

Bob and Tom's passengers came into our lounge in time to see this. One of them looked at me. "What's going on?," he asked.

"The flying school manager is teaching your pilots some Canadian humour."

13/ Butchers

Pelee Island sits in the middle of Lake Erie just north of the international boundary with the United States. It's the most southerly point in Canada, on a parallel with Northern California. The island's other claim to fame is its pheasant hunt.

A pioneer's experiment in pheasant farming left a snowballing bird population marooned on the island. A hunt was organized every fall to reduce the pheasant menace. It was a popular event for hunters who measured success by the number of kills versus the effort expended. Most hunters took the short ferry ride to the island. If they didn't step on a pheasant getting off the boat, they were guaranteed one if they just fired a gun.

When I worked at Pie In The Sky, we landed the occasional charter flight to Pelee's airport. Hector always took them, leaving Roger and me to do the instructing. But on one of Hector's days off, Ursula received an urgent medevac call asking us to retrieve an injured hunter from the island. Roger was flying with a student, so I rearranged my bookings and took the Cessna 172, fresh out of the shop.

The island was about 160 kilometres southwest of Pie. It was refreshing to travel outside the practice area. The weather was good, so I flew low along the north shore of Lake Erie. The farmland rimming the lake was mostly flat and uninteresting, but the water was quite clear. I could see the lake bottom through the shallow water. It was easy to see that a significant change in water level could either eliminate the lake or flood a large part of Southwestern Ontario.

Today the provincial Department of Health arranges all medical evacuation flights. Dedicated helicopters and chartered twin-engined airplanes are on 24-hour stand-by with two pilots, trained air ambulance attendants and medical equipment.

But this was 1972. Patients needing emergency air transportation made their own arrangements. They paid their own way and took what they could get. The uncertainty worked both ways. I didn't know what might be waiting for me at the other end. I had flown a few medevacs in the bush. I knew blood, pain and suffering were not my favourite passengers.

When I circled the island's airport for landing, I could see three men standing on the edge of the gravel strip. I landed short and stopped beside them. A tall, older man in the middle of the group was holding a gauze pad over his left eye. It looked like my kind of medevac. The patient was in one piece and there was no blood showing. His friends helped him to the aircraft.

"Hi there," I called, opening the door on the right side of the Cessna. "Put him in the front seat beside me."

The eye seemed to be the only problem, but my passenger was obviously in pain. I departed immediately.

During the takeoff and climbout, I didn't say anything. The guy constantly shifted the bandage and squirmed in his seat. After we reached cruising altitude, I tried conversation. I thought it might help take his mind off the discomfort.

"Did anyone arrange an ambulance to pick you up at the Pie Airport?" I asked.

There was a long silence before he answered. "No," was all he said.

"I can radio ahead and arrange it," I offered.

"No, I don't want an ambulance," he replied slowly.

I flew a little further. My passenger continued to shift in his seat, pretending to look out the window on his side of the airplane.

"Would you like me to call for a cab?" I asked.

"No," he said.

More silence. We had half an hour to go. I tried once more. "How will you get to the hospital?" I asked.

"My wife will pick me up," he said in a low voice.

"Oh, good," I said, a little more cheerfully than I meant to sound. "I was having trouble imagining you driving to town with one hand on the wheel and the other on the bandage." It was a weak joke.

I could sense the guy was squirming badly now, but I didn't look at him in case he chose that moment to lift the bandage.

"What's your name?" I asked. "I need it for my passenger records." It was true, but I could have asked Ursula later.

"Paul Fitzwater," he replied.

The name rang a bell. "There's a Dr. Fitzwater in Pie," I said. "I've never met him, but he's the government designated pilot medical examiner in the area. Any relation?"

"You could say that," he said.

When I could see Pie in the distance I radioed Ursula to tell her we were inbound. She confirmed that Mrs. Fitzwater was waiting. The patient relaxed a bit with this news. It was then I remembered that Dr. Fitzwater's initial was "P."

"Is it possible that Dr. P. Fitzwater is a really close relation?" I asked.

He smiled a little. "I am Dr. Fitzwater," he confessed.

"Pleased to meet you, sir. I'm the new flying instructor at Pie In The Sky."

"I thought you might be," he said. He sounded like he was warming up to conversation.

"So you don't want an ambulance, because you know the attendants and you're afraid they'll drop you, right?"

"No, no," he said, smiling a little more. "The ambulance guys are first rate. It's the doctors and interns who are butchers. I'd trust the nurses and attendants anytime."

"Well, we can still call them," I offered.

"No, I'd rather not. I'm more than a little embarrassed about this, so I'd rather go in on my own terms," he said.

"Hey, accidents happen. That's why we have hospitals, right?"

"That's the problem'" he said. "This whole mess was no accident. I got a spec of dirt in my eye and rubbed it. I knew better, but I rubbed it. I rubbed it for two days. I'll be lucky if I don't lose this eye." He was getting upset again. "The best I can hope for is a cornea transplant. I've made a real mess of this, just look at it."

"Ah, no thanks," I said, choosing that moment to check for traffic on the left side. "Don't be too hard on yourself. We'll get you to the hospital and get you fixed up." I set up a descent for the airport.

He heaved a big sigh and calmed down a bit. "I suppose I'm frustrated because I can't work on this myself," he said. "I'll have to rely on one of my ham-handed colleagues."

"I guess it's true that doctors make the worst patients," I said.

That made him smile. "That's easy for you to say; you haven't worked with these guys."

"Hey, we could turn around and I could have you in Windsor in an hour," I said, just for fun.

He smiled again. "No. I have to face the music sometime; it may as well be now."

We landed and I taxied right up to the office. Mrs. Fitzwater came out to the aircraft while I helped the doctor down from his seat. She was a small, no nonsense woman the same vintage as her husband.

"My, aren't we a sorry mess," she said looking at the bandage. "I let you out of my sight for a couple days and look what happens."

The doctor turned to me and said, "How far did you say Windsor was?"

"I think you're in good hands," I replied.

I saw them to their car.

"Thanks for your help," the doctor said, shaking my hand. "Maybe some day I can return the favour."

"Well, I don't know. Hopefully I'll never need that hospital. I hear the doctors are all butchers."

14/ Cricket

Susan and I were raised in cities. In the town of Pie we were cultural misfits. We didn't own a pick-up truck, a Citizens Band radio, or a snowmobile. We didn't square dance and we didn't spend Saturday night playing Euchre or watching Hockey Night in Canada. The result was we didn't have any friends. We seemed doomed to remain this way except we owned a horse.

Cricket was a knothead. You couldn't tell Susan that, because a girl's first horse is her greatest love, no matter how many times she gets dumped off. Susan "bought" Cricket when we lived up north. The mare was a former rodeo horse acquired by a stable where Susan worked. After a summer of being ridden hard and put away wet, Cricket was a miserable pile of skin and bones. The stable owners decided to sell her for dog food rather than feed her all winter. Susan traded our tent and camping gear for Cricket and became the proud owner of her very own miserable horse.

Susan was a good rider, especially after a summer of taking tourists on the trail. But when she went out on Cricket, the horse always came back without her. Susan rode English and when the horse was tired of carrying her, she would suddenly plant her front feet at a full gallop and launched her owner out of the flat saddle.

Susan still loved the horse, so there was no question about Cricket moving to Pie with us. My wife was the big bread winner of the family, so I couldn't say too much and didn't. We had Cricket trailered from Paradise to Pie and boarded her at a local riding stable near town.

The monthly fee at Ferguson's Stable included use of the indoor riding arena. Susan saw it as an opportunity to teach Cricket the fine art of English riding in an enclosed area where the horse couldn't run off. She set up a makeshift jump by laying two barrels on their sides and running a pole across them.

I watched while Susan introduced Cricket to the jump. She walked her up to it, let her sniff and then lead her over it, first at a walk and then at a jog. The horse went over each time, not smoothly, but carefully, one leg at a time. Cricket continued to cooperate when Susan got on her and walked her over the jump. Susan was beaming. Cricket's ears were back.

Finally the time came for a run at the jump. It was obvious from a long way back that Cricket regarded barrels as something to go around. She accelerated hard at Susan's urging, but at an impossible last second, she planted her front feet and pivoted. Susan cleared the jump beautifully, without the horse.

They repeated the scene twice. Clarence Ferguson couldn't stand it any longer. The stable owner had been watching the whole time. He walked to the centre of the ring and gathered Cricket's reins while Susan dusted herself off again and felt for new bruises.

Scotsmen and horsemen are never short of advice. Clarence was both. "You know, missy, they say you can't teach an old dog new tricks and they're right. But the shame of what you are doin' is that the mare would love to be onto something else. Do ya mind if I show you?"

Susan didn't know the old Scotsman well, but she'd had enough of the jumping lesson from Cricket.

"No, go right ahead," she replied.

Clarence set three barrels on end in an arena-wide triangle, leading Cricket by the reins as he went around. The horse followed him with an idle curiosity. Then he led her to the far end of the arena and climbed on. He took his time adjusting the stirrups and getting comfortable in the flat saddle. There was something in the deliberate air of the Scotsman that demanded attention. Cricket watched his every move. Her ears were up and pointed toward the barrels.

Finally Clarence grasped her mane in one big hand and let out a whoop that scared us all. Cricket took off like a shot toward one of the barrels. She accelerated to an incredible speed in a short space. They closed the gap to the first barrel in a flash. Cricket executed her familiar plant and pivot and went around the barrel in a blink. Clarence anticipated the motion and stayed with her. They repeated the act to the second and third barrels and then, with another whoop from Clarence, they raced back to the far end of the arena. Cricket slid to a stop and Clarence hopped off.

They walked back to where Susan and I were standing. "I didn't time the run, but what you got here is a championship barrel racer. She's seen better days, but there's still some spark left in 'er."

"Barrel racing wasn't what I had in mind," Susan said politely.

"Well I could see that, but barrel racing is what you bought. We're havin' a club meet at the end of the month. You might practise a little and have some fun."

She did. With coaching from Clarence and Cricket, Susan learned how to barrel race. At the end of the month, she entered the club meet, flat saddle, English riding helmet, jodpurs and all. I saw several cowboys laugh and point when they saw Susan on her boney old horse. They didn't laugh for long.

The referee blew his whistle, Susan whooped and Cricket did the rest. The horse was beautiful to watch. She obviously loved what she was doing. With her ears forward and eyes riveted on each barrel in turn, she dug in with short choppy strides. The turns were the best. Cricket seemed to take the barrels without slowing down. The front feet planted, but the hind legs never stopped digging.

Susan wasn't as beautiful to watch. She still couldn't anticipate Cricket's next weight shift, but she gamely clutched the horse's mane and stayed on to the finish. They won by more than a second in a race that took less than 20 seconds. It was just the Novice Class for first year entrants, but they beat 17 other would-be cowboys and girls of all ages. Cricket tried to bite the judge's arm when he pinned a big red ribbon to her bridle, but Susan stopped her.

Afterward, several club members milled around Susan and her horse, introducing themselves and congratulating them both. I stood back and watched the beginning of new friendships.

When the crowd thinned out, I added my own congratulations. "Well, Tex, you did good," I said, giving her a hug.

"Thank you. I think Cricket deserves the credit, but how did I look?"

"A little like Wild Bill's sidekick, Jingles," I said playfully.

"Oh, thanks a lot. When we win grand prize at the Canadian National Exhibition, we'll pretend we don't know you, won't we Cricket?"

At that point we were approached by a balding fat man. "That horse goes pretty quick for a bag of bones," he said, running a hand over Cricket's ribs. It was a backhanded compliment typical in the horse world.

"Yes, she does," Susan replied. She sounded polite enough, but I could tell by her look, the man was dangerously close to getting decked. Susan wasn't small, and it had happened before.

"Ever think of selling her?" he asked.

"To you?" Susan replied. She was being flip.

"Maybe." He was being coy.

I thought if Susan ever wanted to buy a decent English horse, this might be her only chance to actually get money for Cricket.

"I'll give you 500 bucks for her."

"That's a lot of money for a bag of bones," Susan said.

"I might go as high as 600," the man offered.

"You might, but you won't," Susan replied. "You keep your money and I'll keep my horse."

After the man walked away I said, "He would have gone higher, you know. That may have been your chance to buy an English riding horse."

Cricket was busy nosing her pockets for treats.

"We don't want an English horse, do we Cricket."

15/ Small Town Snow Day

Our Volkswagen looked like a large dessert. It had been snowing all night. I figured flying would be cancelled, but Susan was scheduled to open the dress shop. The road in front of our house was untouched and there were no cars going by. After breakfast we started shovelling the driveway anyway. Soon two snowplows passed, followed by a string of cars. We jumped into the Volkswagen and rammed through the snow left at the end of the driveway to join the procession.

The parade slowly snaked through town, adding and subtracting members as it went. On the way, it occurred to me that the only snow removal equipment at the airport were a couple of rusted shovels in the hangar. The Pie Airport had three kilometres of runways, 50 metres wide, which is the equivalent of six kilometres of highway, plus taxiways, ramp, parking lot and access road. It wasn't a job for two rusted shovels.

I dropped Susan off at the store and rejoined the end of the procession. When the two plows reached the airport, they turned in. The line of cars waited on the road while the plows continued up the driveway, around the parking lot, across the ramp, down the taxiway and onto the triangle of runways.

I pulled into the parking lot. While I was walking to the office, I could see that the snowplow drivers were in high gear. The lack of road-signs and mailboxes had allowed them to speed up. Twin plumes of soft snow streamed from their blades as they accelerated down the runway. They looked like they were having fun. It didn't take them long to clean the airport. They pulled back onto the road and the line of cars carried on behind them.

Hector and Ursula arrived shortly after.

"Good morning," I said, "I was just going to call the students."

"Don't bother," Hector replied. "they know its snowing. Come and give me a hand shovelling the sidewalks."

"Will Ursula call them?" I asked. It made sense to me to phone the customers on bad weather days, not just out of courtesy, but to make sure they had other bookings.

"No. Ursula won't phone them," he said, sounding a little impatient. "If a student sees it's snowing, he should know we're not flying. If he's not sure, he'll phone. If he's still not sure, then let him drive here in the snow and help us shovel the sidewalks."

I must have looked unconvinced so he added, "Ursula knows to make more than one booking for the customers. Calling them just runs up our phone bill."

So with that small town, snow day education, I helped Hector shovel the sidewalks. When we were done, Hector headed for the hangar and Wilbur's special coffee. I went back to the office.

Inside, Ursula was busy with a huge pile of aeronautical charts. She always managed to find something to do. Pie In The Sky was lucky to have her. She wasn't the best looking girl in the world and she didn't know much about airplanes, but she tolerated Hector and did her job efficiently. I enjoyed working with her.

Right now she was snipping the corners off each map.

"Hi, what's with the maps?" I asked.

"I'm sending away for replacements," she said.

"You cut them up first?"

She smiled. "When the Canada Map Office issues new maps, it replaces old stock sent from dealers like us at no charge. Rather than mail the whole map, we just send the corner that shows the chart's name and date."

"I've never worked at a flying school that did that," I said. "I guess they always ran out between new issues. I have another question. Why is the pile so big?"

Ursula blushed. "You know Hector hates paperwork. A couple of years ago, he placed one big order."

The pile begged me to ask, "How big?"

She blushed more, "1,000 maps," she answered.

It was another example of Hector's poor management. Typically, small flying schools stocked a dozen or so of the aeronautical charts covering its area. In a good year, they might sell 50. At the time, they sold for $1.50. As a map dealer, the school paid half price. Hector had ordered $750 worth of charts.

"So you cut the corners off 1,000 maps every time they're updated?" I couldn't believe it.

"It's a good snow day job," she said. I thought she was showing more loyalty than Hector deserved. "This is the third update since his order. We're down to about 850 charts now. Actually it has worked out well. We received a notice with this renewal that says the government is doubling the price on maps as part of a "user pay" recovery scheme. They're selling for $3.00 now, so we make a nice profit."

My jaw dropped. Hector had stumbled into a money-maker. If there were 850 maps left and Pie In The Sky had paid 75 cents each for them, the potential profit by selling them for $3.00 was nearly $2,000.

At that moment, Orval Swick, my first student of the day walked through the door. I immediately felt badly that he had wasted his time fighting through the snow for a cancelled lesson. I cursed Hector for being too stubborn to let me phone him.

"I'm sorry I didn't call you, Orval," I said quickly. "Hector told me our customers stayed home in the snow."

"Is hokay, I come anyvay," the old farmer said, holding up a hand to signal no apology. "I 'ave to get oudda t'e house or Livi, my vife, she drive me crazy. And if she drive me crazy, I drive her crazy. So I come for coffee and be friendly."

"That's fine, I'll join you," I said.

While I was filling my cup, Orval pointed out the window toward the runways. "Look, 'ere comes Jack."

I turned in the direction he was pointing. I couldn't see anyone. There was nothing but snow. I walked over to where Orval was standing. "What are you looking at?" I asked.

"T'e rabbit, I t'ought we see 'im t'is morning," he said.

There was a big rabbit approaching from the beginning of the east/west runway. At that moment a pack of three or four dogs appeared behind the rabbit, hot on his trail.

"It looks like your rabbit friend has a problem," I said.

"Oh, don't worry about Jack," Orval replied, "He run t'ose dogs as long as I come 'ere. T'ey don't never catch 'im yet."

Orval was right. The dogs were running a lot harder than the rabbit, but they weren't gaining on him. We watched them disappear around the corner at the other end of the runway. Orval explained that he thought the rabbit lived in the woods on the west side of the airport. Often when bad weather stopped the flying, Jack, Orval's name for the rabbit, would run through the yards of the houses across the road and collect the neighbourhood dogs.

"Jack lead t'em to airport and run around t'e runways. I t'ink 'e do for fun," Orval said with a grin.

We waited and sipped coffee. Soon the rabbit appeared on our left, turning onto the east/west runway again. The dogs rounded the corner behind him. They were still running like mad, but their tongues were longer and they hadn't gained an inch on the hare.

Orval walked over to the door and opened it to hear the frustrated howls of the hounds.

"Now watch t'is," Orval said.

As if on cue, the rabbit started to speed up. The gap between him and the pack rapidly widened. His burst of speed made the dogs look like they were standing still. Jack shot off the end of the runway heading toward the bush. The dogs knew they were beaten. They slowed to a walk, still on the runway. The barking stopped. Orval closed the door.

"I guess this is a regular occurrence," I said.

"Ya, is best fun in bad veather," Orval said, then added, "I call rabbit 'Jack,' 'cause he is Jack rabbit."

"What did you name the dogs?" I asked. The question popped into my head for no reason.

Orval's expression turned sheepish and he looked at the floor. "How you know I name t'em?" he asked quietly.

"Just a lucky guess," I replied.

I didn't think he was going to tell me, but he finally spoke up, "I call t'em all Hector."

16/ A Stubby Stubby

The Piper Colt was the odd plane out at Pie In The Sky. In the 1960s and 70s, Piper and Cessna were the main manufacturers of training aircraft. The Cessna 150s we operated were all-aluminum, massed-produced, lightweight aircraft incorporating the latest aerodynamic refinements including a long, tapered wing. The little two-place trainer looked modern and was easy to fly. It floated along, giving dozey students plenty of time to catch up.

The Piper Colt was none of the above. It was a 1930's fabric-covered, steel tube design that Piper adapted to the trainer market as a stop-gap airplane while it developed the more modern Cherokee 140.

When I joined the flying school in the early 70s, Colts had been out of production for 10 years. Hector and Pie In The Sky owner John Torrance had been buying Cessna 150s to up-grade the fleet. There was one Colt left. The plan was to keep it for the rental customers who had learned to fly on Colts. The older airplane was cheap to maintain. Wilbur could repair tube and fabric aircraft in his sleep.

The Colt contrasted with the Cessna 150 in more than just looks and design. It had a thick, stubby wing on a short, stubby fuselage. It flew with all the aerodynamic finess of an orange crate. But it was rugged. Steel tubing criss-crossed throughout the fuselage, adding to the airplane's out-of-date appearance, but making it strong.

Because the two types handled so differently, it was confusing for students to fly both on the private pilot course. We offered the college customers a discount on the Colt to keep it flying, but steered the farmer students to the easier-to-fly Cessnas.

Hector liked the Colt. The airplane had good short field takeoff and landing ability, which provided him with the opportunity to show off. If a student drew Hector for a lesson on the Colt, he was always taught short takeoffs and landings, no matter where he was on the course.

The short takeoff technique was simple. The Colt wouldn't fly below 58 mph, so the procedure was to apply full power, keep the airplane straight on the runway and raise the nose at 58. There were only two mistakes a student could make — pulling back on the control wheel too soon or too late. If the nose was raised before 58 mph, the Colt would ride nose high for the length of the runway and run off the end without ever flying. The correction was to lower the nose and wait for more speed.

If the student forgot to raise the nose, the Colt would continue accelerating down the runway and into the next county, still on the ground. It had to have airspeed and a high nose attitude for the thick wing to do its job. At 58 mph, it was like throwing an anti-gravity switch. With its nose up, the airplane eagerly popped into the air.

The decisive "go/no go" characteristic of the Colt is also what gave it great short landing capability. The procedure that Hector demonstrated to students was to cut the power to idle and hold the nose in a level attitude to set the approach. The Colt would sit there, quietly slowing down and developing a wicked sink. With the ground rushing up, the student would feel like he was in a broken elevator. Hector knew from experience that as long as the speed didn't go below 62 mph, he could raise the nose just before the crash and the lift from the extra four mph would stop most of the descent. The airplane would gently plop onto the runway with little forward motion. The Colt's pithy brakes did the rest. The students were always impressed, according to Hector.

The dramatic lesson worked until Hector flew with Edgar. Edgar was a college student who was walking, stumbling proof that academic ability did not guarantee motor intelligence. Hector normally didn't fly with Edgar, but the snowstorm backed up our bookings and forced the need for a third instructor. Hector picked Edgar because it was a lesson in the Colt. He didn't read the telling notes Roger and I had written in Edgar's file and he didn't appreciate the significance of the kid's faraway look. If he had, he would have seen a need for an analytical approach to teaching Edgar to fly.

Hector automatically gave Edgar a short field takeoff and landing lesson. He thoroughly terrorized the student with repeated demonstrations of daring departures and landings. Then he turned over the controls for one circuit of student practise.

On the takeoff Edgar was hopelessly behind the airplane. He didn't pull back soon enough, but with Hector yelling in his ear, he did pull back. The Colt jumped into the air.

For the approach, Hector really got on the poor kid's case. He made sure Edgar slowed the airplane down for him. As the speed decreased, the Colt began its death drop to the runway. The feeling caused Edgar to freeze on the controls, although Hector didn't realize it soon enough. Just before they reached 200 feet, Hector yelled, "Raise your nose!"

Edgar didn't move.

"RAISE YOUR NOSE!" Hector screamed. He grabbed the wheel and pulled back, but couldn't overcome Edgar's petrified grip.

The Colt hit the runway like a wounded duck. I was briefing Phil Patterson in the lounge at the time. I didn't see them hit, but I heard it. The Colt pancaked into the runway with a heavy thud. I looked up in time to see it hovering in the air, mid-bounce. By then its wings were pointed down in an inverted "V" and the wheels were sticking straight out to the sides. The Colt flopped back down, but the image of the airplane looking like a big bird in the middle of a down stroke, hung in my mind.

I yelled at Ursula to call the fire department and an ambulance. I bolted for the door grabbing the office fire extinguisher on the way out. I sprinted to my Volkswagen with Phil Patterson running behind me. We jumped into the car and drove through the gate onto the ramp. Wilbur blasted passed us trailing smoke in his old pickup truck. We followed him down the ramp and onto the runway.

By the time we got to the wreck, Hector and Edgar were already out. They seemed all right. Hector was red-faced and ranting at Edgar who was standing there with his head bowed.

"What'd you think you were doing?" Hector bellowed. "I told you to raise your nose. You could have killed us both!"

I'd never seen Hector so hot.

"Look at the airplane," he continued to roar. "Didn't you hear me?"

"Yes," Edgar answered meekly.

"Then why didn't you raise your nose when I told you?" he shouted into Edgar's face.

Edgar answered quietly but loud enough for all to hear, "I didn't think raising my nose had anything to do with landing the airplane."

A long silence followed Edgar's admission. He thought "raising your nose" meant "raising your nose," not, "pull back on the control wheel to raise the aircraft's nose and keep it from crashing."

We stood there staring at the Colt. It had absorbed a heavy impact and was now sitting on its belly with bent wings nearly touching the ground. Phil Patterson finally broke the silence. "What happened?" he asked.

"That, my boy," Wilbur said, pointing to the end of the runway only 100 metres away, "was a short field landing."

Calling the fire department turned out to be a mistake. Pie's finest, the volunteer fire department, arrived and circled the wreck in two fire trucks and 20 assorted cars and pickup trucks. The farmers and shopkeepers that made up the brigade unrolled hoses, started pumps, laid out equipment and shouted instructions like a well-practised team. The only problem was a lack of fire.

The Colt sat empty and inert on the runway. The fire fighters weren't sure what to do, so they foamed it. They rigged a foam injection system on the pumper truck and creamed everything in a 30 metre radius of the wreck. It looked like someone had thrown a box of detergent into a fountain.

Then the ambulance arrived. The two attendants were on a mission and they were unstoppable. They quickly identified the occupants from the aircraft and bundled them onto stretchers. Hector had only just started protesting when he had been rolled into the van and driven away. He and Edgar were checked over at Pie General and released.

When Hector came back to work the next day he was furious over all the attention that the accident had drawn. He made it worse by describing what happened to anyone who would listen, painting a verbal picture of Edgar frozen on the wheel, driving the airplane into the ground while he, Hector, unsuccessfully fought for control.

This went on for two days but stopped when he saw that week's newspaper, the Pie Plain Dealer. Norbert Schumacher, the paper's reporter, had arrived at the accident scene after the ambulance had left. Norbert had interviewed Roger and taken a photo of the frothy Colt.

A very different story became the front page news. Roger claimed he simply told the reporter that the student had been practising a short field landing, had failed to flare out properly, and had landed heavily. The newspaper article said the Pie runways were not long enough for a Practising Pilot from the college to land a heavily loaded airplane. Norbert reported that after the crash the pilot had been unable to discharge his distress flares properly, but the Pie Fire Department was alerted and had extinguished the fire. Hector wasn't mentioned.

He liked it that way.

Whether Hector was exonerated by the newspaper or not, I knew the accident was the result of his poor teaching technique. I thought the needless loss of the airplane should have a serious effect on Hector's status as the flying school manager. That idea started me thinking of the changes I would make if John Torrance asked me to take over the Pie In The Sky school, but I was counting my chickens before they hatched.

17/ PDQ

The Colt crash turned into a good business move. This was mainly due to Wilbur's efforts. Hector had nothing to do with it, but it let him off the hook.

With help from Roger, Dag Wilson and me, Wilbur lifted the Colt onto a trailer — Roger on one side — the rest of us on the other. We rolled it into the back of the hangar. Wilbur spent the rest of that day exchanging the radio, instruments, fire extinguisher, battery, tires, and all the engine accessories with unserviceable ones from the quarantine cupboard. Then he billed the insurance company $500 for "recovery and storage."

The airplane had been insured for $4,500, the average market value of a Piper Colt at the time. But the Pie In The Sky airplane was worn out. The engine would have been time expired by the next spring and its fabric covering would have failed the next annual inspection.

In 1972, a Colt engine overhaul cost $4,000. To have an outside shop recover the airplane would have cost another $4,000. After investing the $8,000, the Pie airplane might have been worth about $6,000. That's why the number of airworthy Colts was dwindling. Before the crash, John Torrance, Hector and Wilbur had already decided to replace the Cessna the following year and sell it for salvage, about $1,500.

After the crash, the fate of the airplane lay with the insurance company. The adjuster had the choice of writing it off and paying the flying school the $4,500, less $500 deductible, or having it repaired. For $4,500, there was a possibility the wreck was repairable, but we didn't want to wait through a busy winter for it to be rebuilt and returned in the spring with the same runout fabric and tired engine.

The adjuster asked an independant aircraft mechanic to bid on the repairs.

Stefan Wolaski ran a one-man repair shop near London, Ontario. The old Hungarian was a survivor. He had lived through the Nazis and the communists in the old country, and was now surviving Canadian winters, the Department of Transport, and the uncertainties of the aviation business.

Wilbur and Stefan were competitors. They worked in the same business in the same territory. Over the years, they had recognized a worthy opponent in each other and had established a truce based on grudging admiration and mutual mistrust. But for money, the truce could always be tested.

It took Stefan only a few minutes with a flashlight to see the airframe was repairable. He could also see the accessories were junk. He wouldn't blow the whistle on Wilbur with the insurance company because that sort of thing worked both ways.

After inspecting the Colt, Stefan came into the shop and started a verbal dance with Wilbur. "I take it you don't vant to see dat airplane no more."

"I don't mind seeing it," Wilbur said without looking up. He was pressing new "O" rings into an Avenger hydraulic valve at the time. "I just don't want it back."

"Vell, it's vinter time you know. I could use da verk from time to time,"

"Well, we need an airplane that flies, not one that sits in your shop, from time to time." Wilbur replied. He looked up long enough to measure the Hungarian's reaction.

"Maybe I fix it quick?" Stefan offered.

"If you like that airplane so much," Wilbur said. "Bid on the wreck and not the repair. You can dismantle it for salvage."

"Nothing left on dat wreck any good."

"Well, there could be a box of good spares for it around here," the old mechanic offered.

"I don't know how you sleep at night, Wilbur," Stefan said, shaking his head.

"I don't. I stay awake thinking about staying ahead of you."

Stefan smiled. "Okay, I bid on wreck with good parts in box for me."

"Agreed."

Stefan and Wilbur both bid on the repairs, asking over $5,000. The insurance adjuster said "No." He wrote the Colt off and paid Pie In The Sky $3,850, after Wilbur agreed to drop his "recovery and storage" bill to $150. The adjuster then offered the wreck for sale. A couple of aircraft salvage operators looked at it, saw that everything was worn out, and left. Stefan got it for $700. Pie In The Sky was free to look for a replacement.

Dag Wilson, the barn painting salesman who hung around Wilbur's shop, seized the opportunity to offer John Torrance a short-term lease on his Cessna 150, CF-PDQ. He made it sound like a favour. Pie In

The Sky could lease the airplane for six months at $2 an hour.

Dag's Cessna 150 was old. It was one of the original straight-backed, straight-tailed 1950s versions of the airplane. A Toronto flying school had flogged the life out of it for 10,000 hours before selling it to Dag. He flew the airplane a few times, but it needed work. Dag was a talker, not a doer or a payer, so the Cessna slowly sank into the mud where it was tied down. Now it was overdue for an annual inspection which it could not pass.

On the outside, the aircraft's faded orange and white paint was streaked with vertical black marks from sitting in the rain. It looked like an aging, unwashed tiger. On the inside most of the upholstery had rotted away, leaving bits of foam rubber and bare metal. Many instruments were seized from lack of use and the radio was full of water from a leak in the windshield.

Dag's motive for the $2 lease was free maintenance. He knew Wilbur would have to make the old Cessna airworthy before the school could fly it. John knew the airplane was rough, but another new airplane was beyond the school's budget for a now so he signed the lease.

Wilbur sent Roger out to yank the airplane from its tie-down and bring it inside. He exchanged the radio and instruments with better ones from the shop, carefully labeling everything that came out of the airplane, so he could return them at the end of the lease. He did nothing about the paint and upholstery because it met his crop duster standards.

The engine was another story. It was a dog. It produced more noise than thrust. Wear and corrosion had left little compression. When the propeller was flipped by hand, it spun like a child's pinwheel. All four cylinders needed overhauling, so Wilbur sent out the worst one. His theory was that with one good cylinder firing, the others would ride along. He was right. The engine gave one good kick on every fourth cylinder, enough to send it around four more.

Dag visited the shop every day to stick his face into the old mechanic's work and ask when the airplane was going to be ready. A few times I thought Wilbur was going to bury a torque wrench in the salesman's head, but Wilbur stayed calm and always gave him the same answer. "When I'm done."

When the Cessna was ready, Ursula added it to our schedule. Dag booked it for himself the entire first day. Hector was there. The fact that John and Dag had arranged the lease without asking him, bothered Hector. The flying school aircraft fell under his authority and he usually got his way. Seeing the school maintenance budget disappear into the worn out Cessna didn't help.

Hector also knew that Dag was a lousy pilot, because he had taught him how to fly. It had been a tough year of weekly lessons before the salesman barely passed his flight test. He had flown little in the two years since.

"How about some dual instruction first, Dag? You haven't flown for a while," Hector suggested.

Dag mentally grabbed his wallet. "How much is instruction?"

"Dual is eight dollars an hour. I'm available now."

"I was just going to fly around this area," Dag countered.

"You can do that after we're done. I wouldn't feel right seeing you climb into that airplane without a checkout." Hector made it sound like a friendly suggestion. It'll be fun to fly together again, like old times," he added.

"Okay, but just for a little while."

They were gone three hours. Dag was wrung out and complaining when they returned. "That was the Private Pilot course all over again, Hector. I thought you were just going to give me a checkout?"

"I was, but you needed every minute of that, and when you go up this afternoon, I want you to practise more steep turns and landings."

Dag did go up that afternoon, probably not to practise anything but to enjoy having an airworthy airplane again and to do a little sightseeing. When he returned Hector came into the office from the hangar and made out his bill. "That'll be $117," he said.

"What?" Dag exclaimed.

"You owe $117," Hector said calmly.

"That's impossible. You said $8 an hour!"

"That's right, plus $18 an hour for the airplane. We were three hours this morning and you were 2.5 hours this afternoon."

"What'd ya mean? This is my airplane. I owe you $24."

"You own the airplane, but we operate it" Hector said firmly. "I've read the lease. When you fly it, you're renting. It's $18 an hour. Of course you'll get $2 an hour back at the end of the month."

Dag obviously hadn't thought this one out. "You're being hard-nosed," he said. "There's a 30-day cancellation clause. Maybe we'll scrap the lease."

"That would trigger the pro-rated maintenance costs," Hector said, "would you like to see Wilbur's expenses?"

"Come on. Is this any way for friends to talk? I've been a customer here for a long time. Can't we cut a deal? I'd pay as much as half price. What'd ya say?"

"No deal. Full price, less two dollars an hour for the lease. It's fair. You got your airplane back in the air and the checkout may have saved your life."

Dag may have preferred crashing rather than pay the $117. He stood there contemplating whether it would be worth stiffing Hector for the money.

Hector played another card he had up his sleeve. "Tell you what, Dag. I'll sign you up for the Commercial Pilot Course starting today. Then all the money you spend on flying over the next year becomes tax deductible as an educational expense."

The words "tax deductible" were like a miracle tonic. Dag's frown started to dissolve. "You're not kidding?"

"Nope, I'm not. You and I both know that hell will freeze over before you get a Commercial Licence, but for the next year, you'll be on course."

"Okay," Dag said quickly. He sounded like he was afraid Hector would change his mind.

"There's one condition," Hector said.

Dag's frown instantly reformed. "Now what?"

"To officially be 'on course', you have to fly a dual lesson once a week," Hector declared.

It was a lie. There was no such rule, but he made it sound as if there was. "Of course, the lessons will be tax deductible and you'll still get $2 an hour back from the lease."

"Yeah, but once a week?"

"Well, at least a few takeoffs and landings," Hector said. "You may even consider some night flying." It was good salesmanship.

"Okay, where do I sign?"

18/ Qualified

Ursula quit Pie In The Sky at the end of the year. She and her husband decided they had turned the corner on their finances, so Ursula gave notice that she was leaving to stay on the farm and raise a family.

It was bad news, but we didn't know how bad at first. None of us really appreciated the importance of Ursula's work until she left. We found out quickly because Hector did nothing to replace her.

Through December I had pushed him to find someone while Ursula was still there, but he kept putting it off. Finally he said there was no sense looking near Christmas. During the company's combination Christmas and Farewell-to-Ursula party, Hector took me aside. "You find a receptionist," he said.

"Me? Why me? You're the manager."

"Interviewing people bothers me," he confessed. "I'd end up hiring them all."

"Why didn't you say something before?"

He patted me on the shoulder and said, "You'll find somebody."

I was outwardly miffed at being passed the buck by Hector, but I was inwardly pleased for the opportunity to show some management ability. I had an idea that a well-trained receptionist could help a flying school be profitable. This was my chance to prove it.

The next day I called the local government employment office. "Employment Canada, Mrs. Mappin speaking."

"Hi, I'm calling from the local flying school. We need a receptionist. I was wondering if you have anyone we could interview?"

"Well, you'll have to come to the office and fill in an application," she said in a government-issue monitone.

"I don't want a job," I said patiently, "I'm looking for a receptionist."

"Yes, I realize that, but we need a form completed and an interview before we can screen candidates for the vacancy."

So I went downtown and suffered the things that make employment offices famous. I waited in a long line for a long time before being handed a long form. I filled it in and then sat on a hard wooden chair waiting to be interviewed staring at a faded photo of the queen. The experience revived memories of sitting in the public school vice-principal's office the days I got on the wrong side of Miss Meuller, my Grade 5 teacher.

Mrs. Mappin finally called my number. I approached her cubicle and sat in front of her large wooden desk. She was studying my application. I studied her. The woman looked like she was still living in the 1950s. A pair of winged eyeglasses underlined a beehive hairdo piled high enough to be hiding something. Her only make-up was red lipstick that liberally exceeded the boundaries of her mouth.

I didn't know why I was being interviewed. Perhaps Mrs. Mappin wanted to know more about the job opening. She looked at me over the top of the glasses, pulled a Kleenx from a sleeve and dabbed her nose. She replaced the tissue, adjusted a bra strap under the loose blouse and said, "We pride ourselves at Employment Canada."

"I'm glad to hear that," I said. It was an empty greeting and an equally empty reply. I waited.

She looked at the application again. "We should be able to accommodate your request," she said.

"Good," I replied. I waited some more.

She looked up from the form and frowned as if she expected me to be gone. "You may go now," she said, and returned to her reading.

"Thank you," I said. I didn't know what I was thanking her for. I got up and left.

I thought I had wasted my time, but three days later, Mrs. Mappin called back and proudly declared that she was directing three "screened" candidates to the flying school.

Hector took my students while I interviewed in the back office. The first applicant was a teenager straight out of junior high where she must have majored in makeup, backcombing and rebellion. She sat with fire in her eyes and one leg swinging impatiently. Hector would have picked her for the short skirt, but I was looking for trainability. I didn't see it here. The interview was over when she cracked her gum in my face.

The next candidate was a meek, thirty-year-old housewife. Myra didn't have any secretarial qualifications and had never been employed. During our 10-minute interview, she sat with her head bowed and her hands nervously clutching her purse. She seemed nice but I felt obliged to talk softly so I wouldn't scare her. She gave one- or two-word answers to my questions. I thought she might be trainable, but it would take time. I told her that I would let her know.

The last person was a commercial school graduate in his early twenties. He presented himself well and seemed alert and keen. In my mind, there were two things wrong with him; he was fat and he was male. This was an admission of my preconceived notion that receptionists should be female. The fat boy pitched hard for the job, but I knew I'd never hear the end of it from the other guys at the air service if I'd hired him. I hired the housewife.

Myra started the next day. Hector continued to fly with my students while I tried to train her. The poor woman had the personality of wet tissue, but wasn't as smart. She was a zero, a nice zero, but a zero all the same. She appeared to listen to instructions, but they didn't sink in.

I told her to answer the phone with, "Pie In The Sky." When it rang, she looked at me. "Go ahead, answer it," I said.

She picked up the phone and said, "Hello?" She looked at me again and said, "He wants to know if this is pie in the sky?"

By noon she was in tears and I was ready to shoot her. Myra and I agreed she should go home and not come back.

Hector flew with my students while I worked the desk. I placed a classified ad for a receptionist in the Pie Plain Dealer newspaper.

The first call was from Mrs. Mappin. I quickly realized she didn't know who she was talking to. "Don't you know there is a government employment office?" she asked sharply. She didn't wait for an answer. "You're going to receive calls from a hundred unqualified applicants and you're going to waste time talking to them. Meanwhile your tax dollars are paying people here to screen candidates. Now would you like me to send you pre-interviewed personnel?"

"No," I said bluntly. "I tried that last week and you sent me three misfits. Goodbye."

Next, the hundred unqualified hopefuls called. It seemed like a hundred. I spent the afternoon scheduling 10-minute interviews over the next two days. In the middle of this, the fat boy walked into the office.

"I saw your ad," he said. "I think you should give me a chance. I can type, keep books, answer the phone and all the other receptionist jobs. I can also gas airplanes, move them around and clean windshields."

"Fine," I said.

"I'd be good for the school. I can phone customers, drum up more students and push your pilot supplies."

"You're hired."

"I'm also on a diet. I've already lost 12 pounds and I want to take flying les.....; what did you say?"

"I said you're hired. Answer the phone."

He reached over the counter, took a deep breath and set his face in a huge grin. "Good afternoon, Pie In The Sky......No, I'm pleased to say the job has been filled.....Thank you, goodbye."

19/ Fat Boy

"You what?"

"I hired the fat boy," I repeated. Hector had returned from flying with one of my students. "Keep your voice down. He's started already and he's in the bathroom getting water for coffee."

When the new receptionist came into the room, I made the introductions. "Clarence, this is Hector, the flying school manager. Hector, this is Clarence Newsome."

"Good afternoon sir. I'm making fresh coffee. If you'd like to help yourself, I'll complete an invoice for your student and arrange another booking. How was your flight?"

"Ah, fine," Hector replied. He accepted Clarence's handshake with some hesitation and checked his palm afterward. It would be a while before Hector warmed to having a male receptionist.

Later that day, I introduced Roger to Clarence. Roger was neutrally polite. Later I commented, tongue in cheek, that Clarence wanted to learn how to fly and I thought Roger should be his instructor.

"The airplane large enough hasn't been built," was the big man's response.

"He's on a diet," I offered.

"Well, he must have started this afternoon."

"No, he's lost 12 pounds."

"Fine, when he loses 112 more, let me know. In the meantime, you can fly with him."

Our mechanic's reaction contained a remark about Clarence walking through the village where Wilbur had grown up in Newfoundland. "They'd harpoon 'im," he said. "and use 'im to make candles and soap. He'd supply the whole village for the winter."

I countered with, "If they read and washed as much as you do, Clarence could have supplied several villages."

It didn't take long for Clarence to win us over. He hustled. He arrived early, shovelled snow, made coffee, warmed the office and opened the hangar doors. He took good care of the customers and tried to anticipate the needs of the staff. He was pleasant and had a good sense of humour. He quietly instituted improvements in our operation such as phoning the forgetful university students to remind them of their lessons. He washed the airplanes and cleaned the office, neither of which had been done since I had worked there. Every Monday he gave Hector and Pie In The Sky owner John Torrance weekly profit statements that showed healthy growth.

Clarence's hustle paid everyone dividends. The flying school ran smoother and he continued to lose weight. The only negative effect of his efforts was that Hector had to fly. Clarence talked our customers into more frequent bookings, encouraged them to bring friends out to the airport, and with John Torrance's permission, placed learn-to-fly ads in the Pie Plain Dealer. He followed up leads from the ads by mailing brochures and making phone calls.

The result was more business. All three training aircraft were booked and we needed all three instructors. Hector accepted his fate with grace, but he was counting the days until the spring spray season.

He wasn't the only one. Clarence's efficiency added fuel to my idea that the flying school could do much better with a good receptionist and without Hector's backward management style. Now we had the receptionist, I was looking forward to the possibility of being picked to replace Hector when he left to go spraying. I believed I could manage the school very well with someone like Clarence. Time would tell.

20/ Fly By Night

Phil Patterson telephoned the London Flight Service Station to check the weather for our navigation lesson. "Hello. I'm planning a cross-country flight from Pie to Sarnia and London and back, and I need to know the weather."

"It's fine," the flight service specialist said, and then hung up.

"He said it's fine," Phil relayed to me.

"Call him back," I said. "Ask specific questions and don't let him off the hook until you have everything we need, just like you learned in ground school."

The government Flight Service Station at London, Ontario was our nearest source of aviation weather information. There were good reasons why Phil had been cut short. Five specialists worked the station, but only one at a time. During an often hectic shift, they made hourly weather observations, inputed them into the national weather system, and assembled other weather reports, maps and Notices to Airmen from the teletype. They monitored four different radio frequencies and dispatched flight planning and weather information to pilots flying in the area. They did the same on the phone, answering toll free lines from places like Pie, and handled walk-in inquiries from pilots based in London. They were busy.

The FSS specialists could recognize students on the phone by their hesitancy. They were usually patient and helpful, within the constraints of the job. When Phil told me the response to his call, I knew the specialist. The instructors at Pie In The Sky had nicknamed each one. He had talked to Adolf, a gruff tyrant who hung up if there was any pause in the caller's request. You had to nail him with specific questions, ignore his grumbling and not let him go until you had everything. Phil made three calls that day before he had enough information to complete his planning.

Adolf didn't represent a big problem because we included "Adolf response training" in our pilot ground school. We also arranged a class visit to the flight service station and the London control tower, so the students could tour the facilities. It helped them to see that the control tower and FSS staff, with the exception of Adolf, were ordinary human beings.

When we were planning the school's next visit to London, Hector made a suggestion. "I'll put three students in the Cessna 172 and fly over. You lead the car convoy."

I thought it was a dumb idea. The tour was on a Monday evening and night flying was not part of the Private Pilot Course. "You might have trouble selling three of our penny-pinching customers night flying that they can't count on their course," I said.

"Nonsense," he replied.

He was right. He easily sold all three seats.

On the tour night, we met at Pie In The Sky. I led five cars on the one-hour drive to the London Airport. Hector was going to depart after us, but I assumed the Cessna would be waiting on the ramp when we arrived. It wasn't.

The shift supervisor met us at the control tower door and led us up the stairs to the cab. "You're just in time," the man said, after introducing himself. "The air controller is working an aircraft on the VDF."

He gathered us around one of the three seated controllers and explained the situation. "We don't have radar here, so our only indication of an aircraft's location is what the pilot tells us and a readout from the Direction Finder. It's a simple unit that locks onto radio calls to the tower," he said, pointing to a box with a numeric display sitting on the radio console. "It provides the controller with a digital readout of an aircraft's bearing from here."

"VFW, count to three and back for further steers to London," the controller on the microphone said. It was the registration of the Pie In The Sky Cessna 172.

"Von, two, tree; tree, two, von." I recognized the accented voice. It belonged to Orval Schwick, one of the ground school students riding with Hector.

"Turn right five degrees to a heading of 330, VFW, and advise the airport in sight," the controller said.

I thought it was clever of Hector to ask London Tower for a practise direction-finding steer to the airport. It provided Orval with badly-needed microphone time and gave us a chance to see the equipment in operation.

"It seems to be taking him a long time to find the airport," the controller said to the supervisor.

"Okay, make sure he isn't running out of gas and ask him what he can see."

"VFW, London; what is the status of your fuel and what landmarks do you see below?"

The aircraft mike came on. I could hear Hector talking in the background. "Fuel is hokay," Orval's voice boomed over the speaker, "and below is 401."

"So you have lots of gas, VFW?" the controller asked.

There was a pause. "Roger," Orval replied.

"Fine. Highway 401 is five miles south of the airport. You should be able to see it now. Turn to a heading of 340, you're drifting west."

"Roger," Orval said.

"We haven't determined it yet, but the pilot sounds like a novice who has become lost," the supervisor explained to the group. "The controller will be able to direct him to overhead the airport just from the bearings of his radio transmissions."

I suppressed the urge to tell the man I knew the aircraft and gave a negative nod to a couple of others who were obviously ready to do the same. It was a cold night, but beautifully clear. Visual navigation should not have been a problem. I didn't know what Hector was up to, but I was hoping to find out before I spilled the beans.

"VFW, count to three and back again for steers," the controller asked.

"Von, two, tree; tree, two, von."

"You're still drifting west, VFW. What is your heading?"

"Two fort..." Orval started to say, but I could hear Hector cutting him off.

"Two forty, you said, VFW? Are you heading two four zero?"

There was another pause and then Hector's voice came on the speaker, "It's okay London Tower, this is VFW. Thanks for the practise. We're heading back to Pie now. VFW out."

The back of the controller's neck turned red, "VFW, London, do you read?" he said sternly. There was no answer.

"VFW, LONDON TOWER, DO YOU READ?"

Before we could follow the rest of the now one-sided conversation, the supervisor herded us over to the ground controller and launched into an explanation of this function. In the background I could hear the tower controller unsuccessfully trying to contact Orval and Hector. They did not show up for the tour.

After visiting the tower, we went to the flight service station and were greeted by Adolf. I had never met him, but as soon as he opened his mouth, I recognized the voice. I figured it would be a short visit with Adolf saying, "Hi. This is a flight service station. Good bye."

I was wrong. Adolf gave us a painstakingly detailed tour of the facility. He obviously enjoyed a live audience. He explained useless things such as the climatic trends of Southwestern Ontario, solar wind monitoring, and the difference between wet and dry bulb thermometers. The most educational part was when Adolf outlined the main function of the Flight Service Station.

"We're here to help pilots," he declared. "Call us for all your flight planning needs. We will provide all your weather information, will advise you of special aeronautical notices affecting your route, and file your flight plan — all in one phone call."

While Adolf was telling us this, the phone rang continuously. When he finally answered it, he put the caller on hold and continued the tour. As the evening dragged on, I finally told him that we had to go. I'm sure he would have talked all night.

When we arrived back at the Pie Airport, it was very late. I went into the office and saw that VFW's keys and log book were there, confirming that the aircraft had made it back to the airport.

"Sorry we didn't join the tour last night," Hector said as soon as I walked into the office the next morning. He had been waiting for me. "The guys enjoyed the flight so much, we just flew around instead of landing at London."

"Sure," I said. I had my own theories about what actually had happened. As an agricultural pilot, Hector would not have gained much night flying experience. And he always passed the night lessons on to Roger and me, preferring to go home to his family. The result was a rusty night pilot who, I guessed, got a little lost last night, so he used the direction finding steers from London Tower to find the highway and then scoot home. I knew confronting Hector directly would only bury the truth deeper, so I bided my time.

Orval Schwick came into the office a few minutes later. "Gout morning, gout morning," the stocky farmer said cheerfully. "I bring more money. Sorry I run out last night Hector. I not know my share be so much, but vas vort it." As Orval talked, he unfolded several crumpled bills from his little purse.

"I'm glad you enjoyed it," Hector said quietly as he counted the money.

"Ya, I never know night flying so scary," Orval continued.

Hector made out a receipt and handed it to Orval. "Here you go Orval, thanks for stopping by. We'll see you at your next lesson."

"Why do you say it was scary, Orval?" I asked.

Hector tried to end the conversation with a fierce look, but I ignored it and Orval missed it.

"Oh, night flying very bad. Ve all over I don't know vhere. Every-t'ing look different," Orval said. "Hector, he figure it out, but me; I still be up t'ere."

"Yeah, it was a good trip," Hector said. "Thanks for stopping in, Orval."

"Would you like a coffee, Orval?" I asked.

"Ya, good idea," he replied. "I didn't know evert'ing change at night. Towns vere little vinkling lights, and t'e rivers, railroads and t'ings, vere gone."

"You did all right, Orval," Hector said. "I thought you flew very well."

"Lost," Orval exclaimed, "ve vere so lost, I t'ought ve on da moon."

"Yeah, it looks kind of bleak at night in the winter," Hector offered.

"T'en t'a vindows fog up and ve see not'ing. The airplane go zoom," Orval said, using his one hand to imitate a spiral dive. "but Hector he fix. He pull us out chust in time." The hand swooped back up again.

"Yeah, we had a lot of fun," Hector said. He was watching my reaction to Orval's version of the flight.

"T'en ve call on t'e radio. T'e nice man give us directions to highvay. T'en Hector knew t'e vay."

"It was a good experience. I'm glad you came along, Orval," Hector said.

"Oh, I vouldn't miss it for not'ing. I learn lots last night."

"So did I, Orval," Hector admitted, "so did I."

21/ Fighter Pilot

I asked John Torrance about a replacement instructor. All winter it had been assumed that I would carry the school on my own through the spring and summer when Hector and Roger were flying the ag planes. In previous years the training/rental activity had dropped off as the farmer customers disappeared back to the land and the college students headed for summer jobs. But Clarence's efforts had boosted business with the locals to the point where it looked like two instructors could stay busy year round. I had the manager's job on my mind as well, but I didn't mention it at first.

"You're thinking the student load will stay up over the summer?" John asked.

"Yes, sir," I said quickly. The reply sounded more eager than I meant, but it was genuine. After watching Hector stumble his way to profit month after month, I was anxious to show that the school could make real money when he was gone for the spray season.

"Okay," he said, "Let's try it. Do you have someone in mind?"

"No, but I'll find someone." The optimistic reply was based on ignorance. I had no idea how or where to find another instructor. "I'll start looking now."

"Good, but the new-hire will be the first to go if business drops off," John added. "Let me know how you make out," he said, getting up to leave.

"I'd like to ask one more thing," I said nervously.

"Sure, shoot."

"Who'll be running the flying school when Hector isn't here?"

"Well, I certainly hope you will," he said quickly. "You're doing a good job already." Then he saw the look in my face. "I suppose it would help if we made you assistant manager, wouldn't it."

"The title isn't important," I lied. "I just wanted to know if I could make some daily decisions in Hector's absence."

"Certainly. I'll be available, but the farm is busy in the summer. I'd appreciate having you and Clarence look after things. I think assistant manager is a good idea."

"Thank you very much," I said. He hadn't made me the manager, but I felt the assistant's position was the ticket I needed to make my mark on the flying school. "You won't be disappointed."

John shook my hand and left me with a word of caution. "Don't go hog wild. Remember the profit in any flying school business is thin. It doesn't take much to wipe it out."

"Yes, sir, thank you again." I was listening, but at the same time I was planning how to turn the school around.

The first step was another pilot. In the aviation industry out-of-work flying instructors were hard to find, because the instructor rating lapsed when not in use. Flying schools either hired pilots trained in their own program or stole them from a competitor. At Pie In The Sky we didn't have anyone interested or close enough to qualify, so I got on the phone.

"Hello, Larry? Hi, how're you doing? It's your old buddy."

"I'm fine, thanks. Say Larry, I wondered if you're ready for a change. I need someone to come and instruct with me at Pie."

"It's near London, Larry, you know, the 'heartland' of Ontario. We pay top wage here Larry, you'd like it."

The 1973 version of "top wage" was eight dollars per revenue flying hour. An instructor who hustled and worked overtime, could make $8,000 a year.

"No, no turbines, but we fly new airplanes, Larry, Cessna 150s and a 172."

"No, no twins, Larry."

"Yeah, nice talking to you, too, Larry. Keep in touch."

Like most flying instructors, Larry wanted to be an airline pilot. He didn't necessarily hate instructing, but the airlines paid five times as much for half the work, offered free travel, layovers with beautiful cabin crews, a uniform and the aura, prestige and respect, imagined or otherwise, that went with being a pilot on the big jets.

Clarence overheard the call.

"Did you try the Employment Canada office?"

"No, I didn't," I replied sharply. The suggestion brought back the memory of the misfit receptionists sent to me by the local government employment agency. "Don't you think we'd know about an out-of-work flying instructor in this area before them?"

"Yes, but Employment can access all the offices in Canada. If there are any unemployed flying instructors, they'd pay transportation costs for an interview. If you hired from out of town, government pays relocation expenses."

"I didn't know that."

"Did you know if Employment can't find someone, they will assist in training a less qualified person to the level you require?"

"No, I didn't. You're pretty sharp."

"That's my job," Clarence said, "to make you look good."

I called the government office. The same lady from the last time answered the phone. "Employment Canada, Mrs. Mappin speaking."

I told her who I was and what I needed, hoping that she had forgotten about the last time. I had sent one of her choice "pre-screened" candidates home in tears.

"Yes, I remember," she said. She projected her grating voice through her nose. It sounded like a hornet buzzing in a jar. "You're the one who hired through the newspaper. One moment please."

I figured she'd put me on hold until the cows came home, but she was back in a minute. "I don't have anything under flying instructor," she said, "but the computer shows a pilot available in London."

It was probably an ag-pilot. This was crop spraying country. Many pilots worked summers and collected unemployment in the winter. They didn't instruct, wouldn't instruct and couldn't instruct.

"What kind of pilot?" I asked.

"A fighter pilot. It says here he's proficient on CF-100s, Voodoos and Starfighters. Do you have any of those?"

"No, maybe we should just forget this."

"Wait a minute. It says he instructed in the Canadian Armed Forces, was discharged last month and is looking for civilian work. Wouldn't it be easy to retrain this man to be a civilian flying instructor?"

"Possibly, I'm not sure." It was an honest reply. I had no idea whether his military ratings were convertible.

"Well, if you find out, we can help with the cost of his conversion. It gets him off our payroll and onto yours. Would you like me to set up an interview?" she asked.

"Sure, ask him to give me a call." I figured I had nothing to lose.

Jethro Kingsman was 45 years old. He had retired from the Canadian Air Force as a captain the month before. He and his wife decided to settle in London, Ontario after living on military bases around the world over the last 25 years. To supplement his pension, he had gone to the local unemployment office and asked for work as a fighter pilot. It was an old air force trick. He knew the government would have to grant him unemployment payments. After a career of constant high pressure training and travelling, he looked forward to a long rest. A month later, I called his bluff.

79

Jethro sat in our office trying to look angry and unemployable. He came to the interview straight from gardening wearing dirty jeans, a plaid shirt and a frown. But the fighter pilot showed through. He sat ramrod straight and looked me square in the eye when he spoke.

"Look," he said, "I don't want a flying job and you're not looking for a fighter pilot. Why don't we stop pretending? You call Employment and tell them I'm unsuitable. I'll be on my way and you can look for the man you want."

I was inclined to agree with him. I didn't need to work with someone miserable, but I was too stubborn to give in right away. I asked him why he retired early from the military.

"Two years ago I was a Flight Leader in a Voodoo squadron at Comox, B.C. It was hard work. We were always being tested. Besides regular bi-annual proficiency testing on the Voodoo, we had all-weather instrument check rides, aerobatic proficiency tests, gunnery tests, and bombing proficiency every six months. When I finished flying my own check rides, I had to ride with each of the pilots in my flight during their tests. We also flew squadron operations, war games and gunnery competitions. Fly! Fly! Fly! I never had five minutes to myself."

As a young civilian pilot I was finding it difficult to relate to this tale of woe. I hadn't flown anything faster than my grandmother's Buick. The thought of punching holes in the sky with a frontline fighter sounded like the best job on earth. I didn't say anything.

"During manoeuvers on the East Coast," Jethro continued, "I saw search and rescue helicopter pilots sitting around waiting for fishermen to need help. I thought that was the life for me. I applied for helicopter training and got it. I spent 18 months learning to fly whirly birds. The training was intensive, but I knew the payoff. When I was done, I was posted to my old Voodoo squadron, back in Comox. I complained to the commanding officer at the helicopter school, but he said I'd have to take it up with the CO in Comox.

"I reported for duty at the Voodoo squadron and asked what was going on. The CO said, 'You asked for helicopter training — you got helicopter training; now get your ass back in a Voodoo. We need fighter pilots and all your proficiencies have lapsed.'

"That's when I retired. You can only strap into a fighter so many times before you've had enough. I'd had enough."

Complaints or not, Jethro obviously liked talking about his Air Force days. He dropped his fake frown and started to sound like a nice guy.

"When you were instructing, did you enjoy it?" I asked.

"Sure. It's not as hard as being a fighter pilot. All you do is ride along with one hand on the fire extinguisher and the other on the ejection handle."

As I listened to Jethro, I was beginning to like the idea of working with a mature, well-trained professional for the first time in my life. "Why don't you instruct here?" I said.

"Why would I? I'm just starting to relax. I'm enjoying owning a house for the first time. I don't need to work."

"I understand and I don't want to force you into the job. I'll be glad to tell Employment that you're miserable and unsuitable," I said with a smile, "but before I do, hear me out."

"People come to Pie In The Sky because they like flying. There's no pressure here. Compared to squadron life, this is more like a country club." If Jethro had looked around he would have known I was using my imagination, but I barged ahead. "You may find it fun working with us. There's no gunnery practise, no bombing, and we don't fly in bad weather. We pay top dollar in the industry and you can pick your days off."

He moved to the edge of his seat so his old fighter pilot ears could hear me.

"You're still young and healthy," I continued. "Your unemployment benefits will run out eventually and you'll start looking for work, but for us it'll be too late. We need an instructor now. Come and work for us. You don't have to sign up for a fixed length of time. If you don't like it, you can quit."

"You mean I can pick my own days off and quit anytime?" he asked.

"You set your schedule and we book students accordingly," I said. You can quit or be fired anytime."

He though about it for a minute. "I don't have a civilian instructor's ticket."

"The Department of Transport recognizes your military qualifications. It will give you a Commercial Pilot Licence. For the Instructor's Rating, you'll have to learn the differences between civilian and military instructing and then take a flight test. I can train you for that. Employment will pay the training costs and contribute to your salary while you're learning."

He didn't really want to change his mind, but he knew he would. "Do I have to start right away?" he asked.

"Soon."

"I don't have anything to wear for a job like this."

I smiled. "Yes you do. Right now you're dressed exactly like the rest of the staff and all of our customers." I stood up to signal that the interview was over and that he had taken the job. "I'll get you some text books to look at over the weekend and I'll expect you back here at eight hundred hours sharp next Monday."

Jethro grinned and stood up. He accepted my hand shake. "You're on." Then he added, "This is probably a good thing. After a month, my wife was complaining that I was underfoot. She's not used to my being home. If Employment won't pay for the conversion, she probably will. See you Monday."

22/ You're Trying to Kill Me

Jethro's ten thousand high-speed hours in jet fighters had wrecked his ability to fly small aircraft. This was painfully evident during his civilian conversion training. We did it in PDQ, the baffed-out Cessna 150 that Pie In The Sky was leasing from Dagmire Wilson. It was torture — for him.

"I'll fly left seat," I said as we walked out to the flight line. "I'll pretend I'm a student pilot. To start, you fly a couple of circuits to get the feel of it."

"Roger that," he replied calmly.

I sat patiently while Jethro clicked through the checklist for starting the airplane and taxiing out to the runway. It didn't take him long. The man had obviously done his homework and was already becoming familiar with the procedures. It was nice to fly with a professional for a change. I started to relax.

When Jethro was ready for takeoff, he checked my seat belt, called on the radio, looked for traffic and pulled onto the runway. "Are you ready?" he asked.

"Yes sir. Give 'er hell."

He applied full power and was rewarded with the appropriate noise and vibration, but little acceleration. PDQ trickled down the runway like the Little Engine That Could, but might not. The roar was more from protest than power.

A worried crack appeared in Jethro's fighter-pilot composure, but not in his sense of humour. "My aunt accelerates better than this," he yelled, "in her walker."

"It'll go," I replied, "Give it time."

"It'll be dark."

As we gained speed, the acceleration suffered from some law of diminishing return. "Shall I abort?" he yelled.

"No, it'll fly, pull back."

We had reached take-off speed, but Jethro hadn't pulled back on the elevator controls to lift the nose of the Cessna.

"Abort now?" he shouted.

"No, just pull back."

Jethro was thinking Voodoo. The big fighter needed 135 mph to lift off, a speed easily attained with the kick of twin afterburners. PDQ's normal liftoff speed was 60 mph. Jethro passed through 60 mph looking for more. To him it must have seemed like we were barely moving. His right hand on the control wheel held the aircraft on the ground while his left hand tried to shove the throttle through the instrument panel. The engine noise was joined by new vibrations as the lumpy little tires spun faster and faster.

"Pull back," I shouted.

"Not fast enough," Jethro yelled back.

PDQ was now well past its flying speed. The airplane lifted its tail and rolled down the runway on its nose wheel. It began to wobble like a high-speed wheelbarrow. We were running out of runway.

I turned my head and shouted directly into Jethro's left ear. "Pull back, it'll fly."

Jethro lifted the nose slightly. It was all we needed. The airplane popped into the air, but to Jethro we were flying too slowly. He held the nose low, going for more speed.

"You sure this kite will stay in the air?" he yelled.

"Not if you don't lift the nose to clear those trees," I yelled back, pointing at the bush off the end of the runway.

Jethro grudgingly increased the nose-up angle. "It looks like we're barely moving. We must be on the edge of a stall."

"Not even close. Relax and raise the nose more. We're going to be in the next county before reaching pattern altitude."

It was true. Normally when practising takeoffs and landings, a rectangular circuit pattern is flown 300 metres above the ground. Two kilometres off the end of the runway we were at 100 metres.

"The best rate of climb speed is 75 miles per hour," I yelled. We were doing 95 mph and barely climbing at all. The engine was pegged at the redline.

"This is slow enough for me," Jethro replied.

The first turn in the rectangular circuit was usually made at 150 metres. By the time we reached that altitude, the next town 10 kilometres east, was in sight.

"Are you going to turn on the crosswind leg?" I asked.

Jethro looked at me with raised eyebrows. "Give me a break. We're barely flying now. A turn will put us into the ground."

"No it won't, try it."

He did, but not before pushing the nose down and trading some of our altitude to build up more speed. I pointed to the RPM gauge creeping over the red line as the descent unloaded the propellor. Jethro raised the nose again, but not very far.

The flight was obviously making him nervous. I stopped bugging him and let him get accustomed to flying at the slower speed.

It was the widest circuit I had ever seen. When we levelled off for the downwind leg, the airport was barely in sight. Jethro reduced the power, but only enough to keep it below the redline. The speed settled on 105 mph.

At the end of the downwind leg, Jethro turned toward the runway for the approach. He lowered the nose for the descent, but didn't decrease the power. The airspeed built up to 130 mph. Old PDQ had never known such velocity. Every crevice in the airplane shrieked. The plastic windshield groaned and the engine sounded like a Mixmaster after the beaters had fallen out. Jethro finally relaxed.

"Are you going to land at this speed?" I asked.

He frowned. He could barely hear me.

"There are no thrust reversers," I yelled. "no drag shoots or arrester cables. You have to slow down."

He reduced the power by 100 rpm. We lost 3 mph.

"Slower! Slower! Slower!" I yelled.

He reduced the power a little more, but the speed never went below 110 during the whole approach. I saved my voice and waited to see how he was going to handle an airplane designed to land at 50 mph. I expected the landing attempt to result in Jethro trying to force the galloping Cessna onto the runway in a series of ever increasing riccochets off the nose wheel. He fooled me.

With only slightly reduced power and speed, Jethro flared out and eased the nose wheel onto the runway and held it there. The landing was so smooth the only indication that we were on the ground was the vibration of the nose tire rotating at high speed. Then Jethro applied the brakes. Nothing happened. The main wheels were still in the air, a repeat of our high-speed takeoff. The far end of the runway was coming up fast.

"Go around," I yelled.

Jethro obeyed, repeating a shallow, high-speed climbout.

I took over control on the downwind leg. "I'll show you a proper touch and go landing and takeoff," I said.

I turned the airplane toward the end of the runway and reduced the power to idle. The engine noise died. "You want to see a grown man cry, don't you," he yelled. His voice level trailed off near the end as he realized he didn't have to shout.

I smiled and raised the nose on the airplane to slow down.

"Now what are you doing?"

"Slowing down," I replied. The speed dropped to 80 mph.

"We're going too slow."

"Watch this," I said and selected flaps down.

The flaps on the Cessna were large and effective. The speed dropped to 70.

"You're trying to kill me," he yelled.

"No sweat, we'll make it, don't worry."

Jethro sat rigid in his seat. I had never seen anyone clench his teeth and still manage a running commentary under his breath.

"There's nothing holding us up here. If you want to commit suicide, why take me with you? This approach feels like an enema."

Many pilots make lousy passengers, but Jethro was taking it to the extreme. I slowed to 65 mph nearing the runway, flared out, touched down at 55 and stopped. Jethro let out a big sigh.

"Don't relax too much," I said, "I'm going to takeoff."

I applied the power again. Jethro's right hand was pawing for the non-existent ejection handle by his right thigh. We gained speed slowly.

There was always doubt when taking off in PDQ, but this time it seemed worse. We reached 60 mph and I pulled back. PDQ lifted its nose, but the airplane stayed on the runway, rolling in a nose up attitude. We reached the point where I was thinking of aborting the takeoff when we finally lifted off.

"We're not going to make it," Jethro yelled.

"We're okay. It's always close in this airplane." Now he was making me nervous.

The initial climb was barely enough for us to clear the metre high airport boundary fence. It didn't improve. I got a closer look at the trees in the next field than during Jethro's shallow climbouts. The three bad cylinders and one good one in PDQ's engine were struggling for all they were worth. "Swish, swish, swish, bang; swish, swish, swish, bang." The little altitude we gained on the good cylinder we seemed to lose on the other three. There was something wrong.

I looked around the cockpit. Everything appeared to be normal except the airspeed. It read 68 and was not gaining. I looked outside. The flaps were down — all the way. I had forgotten to raise them after landing. I retracted the flaps and the airplane immediately began to climb.

"You testing me or trying to scare me?" Jethro asked.

"Neither," I admitted. "I screwed up. I should have used the checklist — big mistake."

"Thanks a bunch," Jethro said. "When we were scraping the trees, my arse was puckered to my eyeballs."

I gave Jethro control and had him set up for a landing. Over the next 30 minutes he did several touch and goes. Each was closer to the way the airplane should be flown.

When we shut down, Jehtro said, "I wish I was still in the Air Force."

"You don't like this?"

"Oh, I'll get used to flying these things. If I flew helicopters, I can fly anything. No, I was thinking I'd like to take you up in a Voodoo and go supersonic, inverted, under a bridge somewhere. Then we'd be even."

23/ Dead Sea Gulls Don't Fly

Hector and the Pie High School geography teacher arranged to take the Grade 10 students flying. The kids were to observe the local land use during a flight which would form the basis for class discussion.

I thought it was a smart idea. Besides learning more about their area, the students would be exposed to aviation, a good promotional opportunity for the flying school. "That's great Hector, how many students are we talking about?" I asked. I was thinking of 20.

"Sixty-two," he answered proudly.

"Sixty-two!" I yelped. "How are we going to fly sixty-two people in the Cessna 172?"

"We'll use all the airplanes," he replied, grinning. He nodded his head up and down like it was a brilliant suggestion. "I'll fly the 172. You, Roger and Jethro can fly the 150s. It won't take long."

"What do you mean? It'll take forever."

"No it won't. We'll fly 10 minute hops with a five-minute turnaround. It'll be fun."

The scheme reminded me of the sightseeing flights I had done during the fall bicycle rodeo. They turned into nothing but quick circuits of the airfield in my effort to fit them into Hector's ridiculously low price. "How much are we charging?" I asked.

"Five dollars each," he said. He was obviously proud of this too.

At the time we were getting $24 an hour for a Cessna 150 and a pilot. By my calculations we'd be $12 an hour short with the three smaller airplanes. "We'll lose money," I declared.

"No we won't," he said. "What we lose on the 150s, we'll gain on the 172."

It was theoretically possible, and typical of Hector's stubborn optimism. I said no more. I had seen Hector's funny ideas turn into money makers before.

The tour day was beautifully clear, but cold. An overloaded school bus arrived at the Pie In The Sky parking lot at nine A.M. There were sixty-two students plus half a dozen teachers and parent volunteers. The kids streamed from the bus and ran for the office.

Clarence was semi-ready for them. He had moved the furniture back, brought the classroom chairs up from downstairs and hidden the magazines and ashtrays. There was seating for about 30 people. The rest milled around on the little floor space remaining. They quickly discovered that Clarence had locked our two, single-seat washrooms. The only other items to catch their interest were the candy and pop machines which Clarence, the entrepreneur, had filled. He spent the rest of the day handing out washroom keys and making change.

When the school bus arrived, I was waiting beside the aircraft with the other pilots. At Jethro's suggestion, Roger and I had agreed to fly in formation with him during the tours. He said it would be safer flying together than spending the morning constantly looking for each other. It sounded like fun, but my only experience with formation flying had been watching the Canadian Armed Forces Snowbirds make it look easy. Hector would be on his own, since the 172 was faster but took longer to load and unload.

Jethro said he would lead, which meant he would fly the slowest 150, PDQ. Before the kids arrived, he held a short briefing. "There is an important trust required for formation flying; I'm going to trust you to not run into me, and you're going to trust me not to fly us all into the ground. If we all do our job, we'll be fine.

"Now we'll fly in a 'trail right' formation," he explained. "I'll lead on the left with Roger flying behind my right wing and you behind his right wing. Each flight will be a left-hand circuit of the city, so I'll be turning away from you."

As tail end Charlie in the line of two-seat aircraft, I got the tail end kid. He was a little guy who said nothing while I greeted him, helped him in, and showed him how to work the seat belt and door. Each student had been given a mimiographed sheet of questions about the things they should see during the flight. "If I can help you with those questions, let me know," I said. The kid just stared at the instrument panel without speaking.

Right from takeoff, I had trouble staying on Roger's wing. He obviously had never flown in formation either. If Jethro raised the nose on his aircraft, Roger would raise his nose too much, overshoot Jethro's attitude change, and make two more corrections to return to his station on Jethro's wing. This left me with six delayed and exaggerated reactions for every one of Jethro's changes in pitch, bank, and power. I spent the entire flight sawing madly on the controls. The visual result was a three-dimensional crack-the-whip. Physically it was like riding a mechanical bull.

We had taken off from runway 27. Jethro turned left toward the city, flew a half circle around it and landed straight in on the same runway. We were exactly 10 minutes.

My passenger said nothing during the whole flight. I had been so busy staying in the formation that I hadn't had a chance to look at him until after we had landed. He was wide-eyed and green. When we came to a stop on the ramp, he struggled to undo his seat belt with one hand and clawed for the door with the other. He half scrambled and half fell out of the airplane. He was clutching a rumpled sheet of unanswered questions as he staggered away on rubbery legs.

My next passenger was the Chatty Cathy type. She babbled excitedly about this being her first airplane ride while I helped her settle in the seat and put on her belt. "I'll be busy flying the airplane, so I won't be able to help you look around and answer those questions," I said.

"That's okay," she said with a nice smile, "I'd rather you flew the airplane."

While we were taxiing out, the Bob and Tom Show landed in the King Air. "Well if it isn't the three little ducks, Huey, Duey and Louey," Bob said on the radio as the turboprop rolled onto the ramp. "Where is Hector, the mother duck?"

"Right behind you," Hector replied from the 172 over the city.

"Say, Hector, what do you get when you cross a flying school manager with a gorrilla?" Bob asked.

"I don't know," Hector said.

"A retarded gorrilla. Hee, hee, hee."

My passenger giggled. "It must be fun being a pilot," she said.

"Laugh a minute," I replied.

She stopped talking right after takeoff. My formation proficiency improved slightly, but continuous multiple corrections were still necessary. It was an uncomfortable ride.

I looked at Chatty Cathy after landing. She smiled weakly through clenched teeth. When we stopped, she tried to bolt through the door with her seat belt on. I helped her out and she ran for the office without thanking me.

Passenger number three was Mr. Cool. He sauntered up to the aircraft like he was on stage. His jean jacket was fashionably open despite the cold and he didn't smile.

"Hi," I said, "The flight may be a little rough. The air is smooth, but the pilot isn't. If you feel the need, there's a little white bag in the pocket behind your seat."

He glared at me as if I had questioned his gender. He climbed into the Cessna without answering.

I managed to reduce the formation corrections to a steady ripple of movement, but it was still too much for Mr. Cool. Too much pop, too many chips, too much bottled-up excitement and too many airplane gyrations translated into a boot, instructor jargon for throwing up. Fortunately he signalled with a couple of dry-heaves. It gave me time to reach into the pocket behind him and pull out a bag. I snapped it open and shoved it under his face without taking my eyes off Roger's wing.

Once he started I thought he'd never stop. He wretched for the rest of the flight. I felt badly for him. There is nothing less cool than losing your cookies. When we landed, I apologized for the rough ride.

"What do I do with this?" he asked. I looked at him. He was holding the bag precariously in both hands. It was so full there wasn't room to fold it over at the top.

"Hang on to it," I replied.

"I can't let the other kids see me with this," he pleaded.

I looked at him again. He was nearly in tears. "You're right," I said. "Open the door and toss it out here."

We were just pulling off the end of the runway. I stopped the airplane and reached over and opened his door. He didn't need a second invitation. It was a little messy. The wash from the idling prop blew some of the contents onto his sleeve, but the kid managed to get most of it out the door.

Bob and Tom took off in the King Air as soon as we were clear of the runway. They had dropped passengers at Pie and were heading back to Ohio. Heactor landed following their departure. Before I shut down on the ramp I could hear Hector calling the King Air on the radio.

"Say Bob, did you guys clobber a sea gull on take off?"

There was a short silence. "Is this an attempt at a joke, Hector?" Bob asked.

"No I'm not kidding," Hector said, "there's a very dead sea gull in the grass off the end of runway 27. It wasn't there on my last flight."

"We didn't hear anything hit," Bob said, then he added, "It would be a bad joke, Hector."

"Suit yourself," Hector said, "I'm just telling you there's fresh kill by the runway."

"Okay, we're coming back," Bob sighed. "We don't really have time for fooling around, Hector."

"Maybe it wasn't you, but it wasn't likely one of us."

Hector sounded sincere and he was probably right. The local sea gulls had plenty of practise dodging Cessnas. They knew when to veer out of the way at the last second. It was only when a faster airplane like a King Air came along that they sometimes misjudged their break.

After I shut down, Mr. Cool calmly climbed out of the aircraft and sauntered away. His face was a little pastey, but his composure was restored.

Chatty Cathy must have told everyone in the terminal building that tail-end Charlie was the one to avoid. The three passengers for the next flight raced to climb into the first two aircraft. The loser started walking back to the office, until the geography teacher yelled at her and pointed in my direction. She argued with him for a while, but he prevailed.

"I'm getting better with each flight," I said hopefully, holding the door open for her. The young teenager ignored me and climbed in without comment.

We had to wait a minute for the King Air to land before taking off. This flight was better. By keeping less than perfect station, I reduced the number and magnitude of corrections. My passenger sat rigid, but I had time to explain some of the aircraft instruments and point out a few landmarks during the flight.

After landing, I looked for the dead sea gull off the end of the runway. I couldn't see it. When we taxied to the ramp, there was a group standing by the King Air. Bob and Tom were talking to Hector, Wilbur and the geography teacher. Wilbur handed the teacher the dead sea gull on the end of a stick. It was the sick bag.

I shut down and climbed out of the Cessna in time to hear the teacher open the door to the lounge and demand, "Okay, who threw this out of an airplane?"

I walked over to the King Air. Bob was dancing in front of Hector and flapping his arms. "Sea gulls have wings and feathers," Bob said to Hector. "Barf bags don't fly."

Hector smiled, "How was I supposed to know it was a barf bag you hit?" It was a weak joke, but one of Hector's best.

"Sorry about that Bob," I said. "It was my passenger who tossed that out at the end of the runway."

Bob didn't seem upset. My confession launched him in a different direction. "Tom," he said to his partner, "was it rough when we were flying?"

"Nope."

"That's what I thought. A clear calm day was had by all except the three little ducks. Are these poor kids paying for this?"

"We were practising a little formation," Jethro offered.

"Formation," Bob hooted, "is that what that was? A Pie formation must be any three aircraft in the air at the same time. Well, good luck guys. Come on, Tom. Let's get back to work."

The two American pilots climbed into the King Air and the rest of us started walking back to our aircraft. "Send me over a passenger, will you?" I said to Jethro.

He looked puzzled until he spotted the two kids fighting to get into his airplane. "Okay," he said.

24/ Don't Try This at Home

Jethro fit in well. He had been raised in a small town, so he adjusted easily to the "life in a fish bowl" aspect of working in Pie. He was the same age as our farmer customers, and the college students got a kick out of his 50s crew cut hair. He bridged the generation gap with colourful expressions brought from the military. "Patterson, don't tell me you forgot your map again. A map is a pilot's tool. If you went to a whorehouse, would you forget your tool?"

"No sir, I wouldn't," Phil Patterson answered with a grin, "and at a whorehouse, I wouldn't need a map."

Jethro beat his fear of slow flying by pretending the training aircraft were helicopters. "They vibrate just as bad, won't carry any more load, and seem just as unsafe," he said.

"Fine," I replied, "but you'll discover they're not helicopters when you try a hover."

Hector was happy that Jethro had joined the Pie In The Sky staff. He assigned his students to Jethro and disappeared into the hangar to help Wilbur ready the spray aircraft for the fast approaching spring.

The Pawnees were first. Hector and Roger would fly these locally, spreading fertilizer during April. Then in May, Hector would fly one of the monster Avengers to New Brunswick in formation with Frank and Leon to spray the forests. Roger would continue flying a Pawnee on local spray contracts.

In early April, Pie was the site of the annual ag plane calibration meet. This two-day, weekend event was sponsored by the Department of Soil and Sea, the government office that regulated aerial application in the province of Ontario. The meet was held every spring to give ag operators an opportunity to check the flow on their spray systems. It was a voluntary event, but Soil and Sea would not give government spray contracts to operators who did not attend.

About 20 ag planes flew into the Pie Airport on the Friday. It was a negative learning experience for our student pilots. None of the ag flyers used a radio on arrival and few of them bothered with the active runway. Instead, they landed on all runways and taxiways, in all directions. They parked everywhere. Hector, Leon and Frank shuttled them downtown to the Pie Hotel.

At eight o'clock the next morning, four government representatives set up a seminar in our basement classroom under the terminal building. They planned to start with a review of chemical application regulations. Nobody showed up.

They came upstairs for a coffee.

"This happened last year," one said.

"Yeah, but they promised this year would be different," replied another.

"Well it looks like it's not."

The pilots in question had conducted their own seminar in a bar the night before. The first few arrived at the airport around 10:30 wearing sunglasses. It was cloudy. They were speaking softly and obviously carrying big headaches.

By noon there were enough participants to run the calibration tests. Jethro and I were the only instructors available, but I stole a few minutes to drive my Volkswagon out to the end of the runway to watch.

The set-up was simple but clever. The government reps rigged a long piece of white string about a metre above the ground across one of the runways. The pilots flew over the string spraying purple-coloured water. A Soil and Sea worker clocked the aircraft's speed with a hand-held radar gun. The pass deposited purple dots on the string. The string was then run through an electronic scanner that counted the dark spots. The count and the airplane's speed were matched on a chart which determined the nozzles' actual flow rate.

Paul Gagnon was the first pilot to fly a run. Paul was the grandfather of spray pilots in Ontario. He was big, bald and barrel-chested. He looked like Mr. Clean's uncle. Paul had partied all night with the rest of the pilots, but he was voted the most capable to fly first. He owned a beautifully restored Boeing Stearman, a 1930's biplane used as a military trainer in World War II. You could eat off Paul's airplane but he wouldn't let you. You might spill something.

I was out at the calibration rig when Paul made his first pass. The big yellow biplane gleamed despite the cloudy weather. He headed right for everyone standing beside the runway and not at the string. I thought he was going to turn at the last minute, but he didn't. The spray came on and Paul coated the S & S staff, their equipment, their white van and my white Volkswagen with purple dots.

"He did that last year," said one of the workers.

"He promised not to," replied another.

"He lied."

"How do you get the dots off your car?" I asked one of the workers.

"You don't," he replied. "You either go to the ramp and wash your car in the purple solution, in which case you end up with a purple car, or you park it in the sun and in about three years, the spots will fade."

I drove my newly spotted Beetle back to the office and went to work. I spent the afternoon teaching students to look in 360 different directions for air traffic before taking off. Every student flying that day earned a healthy respect for the vagaries of operating from an uncontrolled airport invaded by cowboy pilots.

Toward evening the sky cleared and the wind died. My last student was Justin Hanover, who was working to finish his Private Pilot Licence before the school term ended. When we returned to the office, there were 20 ag pilots drapped around the lounge half-heartedly listening to the Soil and Sea staff lecture on the day's results. One of the pilots looked past me at the windsock outside.

"Hey, the wind's dropped," he said in a loud voice.

Twenty near-lifeless bodies suddenly jumped out of their chairs. Phil and I had to step aside to avoid being run over as they charged the door. Hector was among them.

"Hector, what's happening?" I asked

"Water skiing. We're going water skiing," he said as he continued out the door.

I could see the other pilots were headed for their airplanes, but I didn't have a clue what he meant. "Do you want to see what he's talking about?" I asked Justin.

"Sure, I'm game."

"Okay, let's go."

That one flight unravelled much of what Justin had learned about flight safety. When we got to the Cessna 150, half the ag-planes were already started and moving. "Skip the pre-flight, Justin," I called out, "We just flew it. Climb in."

By the time we buckled our seat belts, half the ag-planes were airborne and the other half were accelerating down the taxiways and across the infield. "I'll get us going," I said stabbing at the switches and controls, "You handle the radio."

The radio work was to keep him busy while I ignored the checks, started the engine and taxied out to the nearest runway. "We'll depart runway 21," I said. "I'll do the takeoff and I'm ready now. You make the radio call."

He did. There were no other pilots on the frequency. We took off and followed the fleet of ag-planes disappearing southbound.

We arrived at the lake in time to see the 20 airplanes flying in a loose "V" formation parallel to the shoreline. They were close to the water and descending. As we got nearer, I could see several of the aircraft had contacted the water with their main tires. Spray streamed back from each wheel leaving tiny twin wakes behind. By the time we were overhead, all the aircraft were "skiing" their tires on the water. It was an incredible sight. The mirror smooth lake was being split by the formation of ag-planes riding across the surface.

"Is that legal?" Justin asked.

"I don't know, but I guess if we have to ask, then it probably isn't. Do you want to try it?"

I was kidding, but the reaction was perfect. I could see by his changing expressions that the sensible side of his personality was struggling with the daring side. "I don't think so," he said.

"It's all right," I said, "I can see you're nervous."

Justin was sharp. "I'm nervous because you're flying and I'm not sure you could handle that."

"You're right."

25/ Aircraft Calling Pie

By mid-April, everything was in place. I took over the Pie In The Sky flying school as assistant manager and was ready to demonstrate how it should be run. Hector and Roger were still around, but were spending long hours aerial fertilizing with the Pawnees.

Jethro and I were extra busy flying with their students as well as our own, so the key to my success as assistant manager was Clarence. He made the managing job easy because he worked beyond the receptionist's job description. He handled our advertising, coordinated maintenance with Wilbur, ordered fuel before we ran out, deflected salesmen and charted our growing profits.

On the first official day of my new position, Clarence was there when I arrived at work. "Good morning boss," he said, "I've got news."

His tone made me stop and look at him. He didn't look happy. "I don't think I want news," I replied.

"I'm leaving," he said.

I was right. I didn't want news. I was instantly depressed. He had to be kidding. "I'm sorry, Clarence, but you can't leave."

He smiled weakly. "I'm sorry too, but a good opportunity came along and I'm going to take it."

"What about your flying lessons?" I asked. Anything was worth a try.

"On hold," he replied.

"What about the flying school?" I asked.

"It'll survive. You'll find someone else," he said. "I've prepared an ad for the newspaper and I can call the Employment Canada office if you like. I can even interview the prospects. I'm not leaving until Friday."

"Friday," I exclaimed, "This Friday?"

"Yes, this Friday."

Thinking about it later, I realized I should have anticipated his leaving. I had believed the very keenness Clarence had displayed in wanting the job and the subsequent enthusiasm he maintained at work, meant he would stay at Pie In The Sky forever, but those same things were his reasons for leaving. Clarence was too good to last in a small town flying school.

"How about a raise? A little now and a little more later?" I asked.

This was like closing the barn door after the horse had escaped, but I thought it was worth a try. The flying industry paid receptionists minimum wage. This was based on the belief that anyone could answer a phone, make bookings, post invoices, smile at customers and make coffee. The fact Clarence did much more had never been reflected in his salary.

"No, I'm quitting because my new job has more scope. I cut a deal at my old business school. I'm going to do promotional work for them. I hope it leads to more opportunities."

"You're not helping my debut as assistant manager," I said.

"You'll do fine," Clarence said with a smile. "When I'm rich and famous, I'll come back for flying lessons. I'll be your best customer."

"You're telling me to stop wasting my breath."

"Right. So what'll it be, the newspaper or the Employment Office?"

"The newspaper," I replied. "Call the ad in now and it'll appear this week. Maybe I can stick you with screening the calls and training your replacement."

"Sure, boss, no problem."

The prospect of losing Clarence put a big hole in my plans for Pie In The Sky. In the short term, my revenue contribution to the company would be reduced while I spent time working with a new receptionist, but the long term impact would be worse. It was unlikely I would find another Clarence.

Over dinner that night, I told Susan that Clarence was leaving.

"What are you going to do?" she asked.

"Clarence placed an ad in this week's Pie Plain Dealer," I said without much enthusiasm.

"What qualifications did you list?"

"I didn't," I replied. "The ad just indicates a position is open for a receptionist/bookkeeper."

"So you need someone with communications skills who can count to ten," she said with a grin. I liked the way she simplified things.

"What I want is another Clarence," I replied, "but I'll probably end up with a useless dimbulb of a chairwarmer. I'll have to do most things for her."

The "her" was the mistake. "So you want a male, but you expect to be 'stuck' with a female," Susan said, rising in her chair, "and she will, of course, be useless."

Her face flushed and her hair bristled. "Male or female is not the point," I said quickly. "If you saw the people I interviewed last time, you'd understand."

"They were females?" she asked.

"Yes," I said tentatively, "But that has nothing to do with it." I was lying to save my skin, but she didn't have to know.

"You're lying," she retorted. "Would you hire a female if she was as good as Clarence?"

"Gladly," I said. "I just don't think I'll find another Clarence, male or female.

"What makes Clarence so good?" she asked.

"Well, it's the extras. Anyone can learn to answer a phone and post invoices, but Clarence does more."

"Like what?" She was being persistant.

"Well, for instance, he cleans the aircraft and the office, writes a newsletter and phones customers to remind them of their bookings."

"So you need a maid with communication skills who can count to ten," she said.

"Well, its more than that," I laughed. "With Clarence there, the rest of us don't have to do anything but fly. He runs the rest."

"So you are looking for a maid with communication and organization skills who can babysit."

She was probably closer to the truth than I cared to admit.

"The main thing is that Clarence works with his eyes open and does a good job without being told what to do."

"Okay," Susan said, "All of the above and the ability to read minds as well."

"Sure," I laughed. "Where do I find someone like that?"

"Right here," Susan replied. She wasn't laughing.

The realization of why she was so interested in Clarence's leaving washed over me. During our conversation, Susan had decided she wanted Clarence's job.

My initial reaction was to buy time and collect my thoughts. "What do you mean?" I asked.

"Me," she said, "Hire me to replace Clarence."

"You already have a job. What about the dress shop?"

I was stalling. My question didn't reflect what I was thinking. I knew Susan could do anything she put her mind to, but I wondered if she and I could work together while she learned a new career.

"The shop will survive without me," Susan said. "My job is not that difficult. My boss can hire one of the dimbulbs you were talking about."

"I thought you liked working there."

"Not really," Susan replied, "I originally thought it was a lady's fashion store."

"And it's not?"

"Not really. Pie is about as far as you can get from a 'fashion centre.' I spend a lot of time complimenting the looks of farm wives in print sacks. I'm tired of it."

I obviously had not been paying attention to Susan's part of our evening conversation.

"Clarence's job doesn't pay much," I said. As assistant manager at Hymie's, Susan made about three times what I could pay her at the flying school. That thought gave me visions of eating macaroni and cheese, seven days a week.

"That never stopped me before."

She was right. Her job before coming to Pie had been cleaning stalls at a riding stable for $5 a week. "I'll think about it," I said.

She didn't let up. "What's the matter? Do you think I'm just a useless dimbulb chairwarmer?"

This was my chance to regain control of the conversation. "Yes," I said. "That's why I married you. I couldn't live with someone who displayed initiative or intelligence."

"You creep," she said. At the same time she got up from the table and charged around to my side. "If you're going to talk like that, you can stuff the job," she said. She grabbed my shirt with both hands. I didn't know if she was going to rip it off or kiss me passionately. "I think we could work well together," she continued. "I'm sick of the dress shop. Say the word and I'll quit tomorrow."

"You're right. It might be fun," I replied.

"Whoopee," Susan yelled in my face. Then she leaned back and ripped my shirt.

Susan gave her boss two weeks notice. This meant that Clarence left the flying school before he could give her any on-the-job receptionist training.

Susan's only claim to aviation was being married to a pilot. Her limited exposure to airplanes had been riding with me on a few pleasure flights. She hated it. Flying made her sick. Susan's view of airports had often been from her knees, in front of a toilet. I was a little worried about how she would take to the flying school.

I shouldn't have been. Susan was neither timid nor stupid. A career in retail management had left her trained to deal with people. From her start at Pie In The Sky, Susan was in control.

A simple example was how she handled Hector when he sauntered into the office on an afternoon too windy to fertilize. I was showing Susan how to fill in the aircraft log books. Hector was looking for a fresh cup of coffee. The stuff in the pot had obviously been cooking for a while, something that never happened during the reign of Clarence.

Hector didn't know Susan well, but he didn't let that change the fact that he had never made the coffee. "Susan, could I get you to fix coffee?" he inquired politely. "We usually keep the pot fresh for the customers."

Before I could intervene, Susan looked at Hector, sized up the situation, and said, "Hector, there are no customers."

"Well, you never know. One could come in any moment. We keep it fresh just in case." He grinned hopefully and nodded his head up and down.

She looked him in the eye, but kept a friendly edge to her voice, "Hector, if a customer comes in, I'll gladly make coffee," she said. "In the meantime, I'm doing log books. If you'd like to help, either make the coffee, do these log books, or go back to the hangar and tell Wilbur that TWX will be due for a 50-hour inspection in three hours."

It was great. She had put him in his place and given him an out.

"I'll go tell Wilbur about the 50 hour," he said.

"Thank you," she replied.

"Was I too hard on him?" she asked when he had gone.

"Not a bit," I replied.

Susan dispatched the two-way radio with the same direct efficiency. It's difficult for anyone to understand the rapid-fire pilotspeak on the office unicom. It's especially hard when the listener is unfamiliar with the aeronautical communication jargon. It is impossible when they are trying to learn the receptionist's job at the same time.

Susan simplified the problem by memorizing a short reply that I composed for her and used it on everyone. Whenever she heard the phrase, "Pie Unicom," she replied, "Aircraft calling Pie. Runway your discretion. Watch for other traffic."

It didn't always work.

"Pie Unicom, November Victor Charlie 10 east landing, request airport advisory."

"Aircraft calling Pie. Runway your discretion. Watch for other traffic."

"Pie Unicom, NOVEMBER VICTOR CHARLIE REQUESTS AIRPORT ADVISORY."

"Aircraft calling Pie. Runway your discretion. Watch for other traffic."

"PIE UNICOM, NOVEMBER VICTOR CHARLIE REQUESTS YOUR ACTIVE RUNWAY AND TRAFFIC!"

"Aircraft calling Pie, listen up, because I'm only going to say this once more. The dumb receptionist doesn't know the runway and we often have other traffic, so keep your eyes open."

There was a long pause, "Oh, okay. Thank you Pie."

"You're welcome."

Susan applied her directness, the "Susan factor," to everything. The government required that an entry be made in each aircraft log book every time it flew. I showed her how.

"Enter the time up and the time down from the daily flight sheets. That gives you the total air time," I explained.

"Yes," she replied slowly, looking at me like I was dim.

"The next column," I continued, "is the total flight time. That's the total time from when the aircraft starts moving from the ramp under its own power, to the time it stops moving under its own power back at the ramp."

"So it includes the time going to and from the runway?" she said, patiently.

"Right," I replied.

"Why do they call it 'flight time'?" she asked.

"I don't know."

"So the pilots keep track of the time out, time off, time down and time in, on the daily flight sheets, and I transfer them all into these books?"

"Right."

"That's stupid," she said.

I suggested she do it anyway. It was required by law and I didn't want to encounter the wrath of the government, God and the queen.

"How long does it take to go to the runway and back?"

"About five minutes," I said.

"Fine, you enter times up and down on the flight sheets and I'll add ten minutes for each flight to the 'flight time' column," she said. "That'll save time and reduce the likelihood of my committing mathematical errors."

"And you'll take care of the government, God and the queen?" I asked.

"Yes," she replied.

"Suits me."

26/ Poetry in Motion

In the middle of Susan's first week, it rained three days. The washout meant lost revenue for the flying school, but it gave me time to teach Susan the receptionist's job. The bad weather also put Hector and Roger behind on aerial fertilizing the local winter wheat. Each rainy day added farmers to their customer list as it became too wet for ground spreaders.

On the first dry day, Susan and I went to the airport early. I was anxious to make up some flying time. Hector and Roger were already there, but Hector was in the middle of sending the big pilot home. Roger had the flu and looked like death.

"Go back to bed," Hector said to him, "I'll get Wilbur to fly for you."

It was the first I had heard that Wilbur could fly. I was surprised. The old mechanic didn't look like a pilot. Wilbur was the original 90-pound weakling. Frank once said that Wilbur was so ugly that, "when he was born, the doctor slapped his face before he realized it was the wrong end."

But fly he did. While I was pulling out and gassing the school aircraft that morning, I was able to watch Hector and Wilbur work. It would be dificult to imagine any two people doing the same job with identical aircraft as differently as those two.

When Hector returned for another load of nitrogen fertilizer in his Pawnee, he could be heard from a long way off, approaching the airport with the propeller tips wailing at full revs. It was obvious that he was in a hurry. He dove for the runway and chopped the throttle. The engine popped and banged from the sudden power reduction. He forced the airplane onto the runway in a series of hops, skips and tire chirps. As soon as he had the Pawnee slowed down, he kicked the rudder and goosed the throttle to swing around and roar back to where the loaders were waiting.

The bags of fertilizer were piled on a flat bed truck parked beside the runway. Hector charged the truck and spun the Pawnee around. As soon as he had shut down, he dropped the fold-down door, climbed onto the wing, and leaned forward to snap open the hopper lid located ahead of the windshield.

There were two loaders hired for the season. They relayed the bags from the truck to Hector who stood on the wing and dumped each one into the hopper. As soon as the airplane was full, Hector jumped back into the cockpit, started the engine and slammed the door. The loaders turned and ducked as the airplane's low wing sliced over their heads. The blast from the prop covered them with dust kicked up from the taxiway as Hector goosed the throttle and roared down the runway into the air. It looked like hard work, but I was impressed by Hector's speed. The whole reloading operation had taken about five minutes from landing to takeoff.

When Wilbur approached for landing, I couldn't hear him coming. He glided to the runway with the Pawnee's engine shut down and the prop windmilling. He slowed down in the air and did a "keyhole" landing. This involved angling across the runway from left to right during touchdown and braking hard enough to keep the tail in the air. As the airplane reached the right edge of the runway, Wilbur swung it around to the left in a runway-wide arc, tail still in the air. With the prop stopped, he carried enough momentum to taxi back to the truck and swing around beside it.

While Hector was quick, Wilbur was smooth. When Wilbur's aircraft was full, he secured the hopper, climbed in, started up, and closed the door, all in one motion. There was no hurry and jerk, and there was no wasted movement. Full power was applied with the prop blast pointed away from the truck. As the loaded Pawnee gathered speed going down the runway, Wilbur lifted one wing and entered a turn toward his field on takeoff. He was beautiful to watch. His flying made Hector look like a demolition derby driver.

In the time it took me to pull out and gas three airplanes, Hector had flown three loads. Wilbur did four. The two ag pilots flew all day. When I returned with my last student at dusk, Hector was plopped in a chair like he'd been shot. He was sound asleep. I finished with the student and tiptoed past him to put the airplanes away.

When I taxied the Cessna 150 into the hangar, I could see Wilbur had Hector's Pawnee on jacks and was changing the brakes and tires. I climbed out and walked over to him. "Can I give you a hand?" I asked.

"No thanks," he said. "I just have to put this tire on and I'm finished."

"You guys worked hard today," I said, "it was fun watching you."

"Yup. These days make up for the goldbricking in the winter."

"I didn't realize that you could fly. You're a good pilot. You were outflying Hector about four trips to three."

"Well, don't make too much of that," Wilbur said, putting the cotter pin in the axle. "Hector's a good pilot. I've just been doing it longer."

"Well, I wouldn't bet on Hector becoming as good as you."

"Don't be too hard on him. We all bring what we can to the job," he said.

"You did the majority of the fertilizing and now you're fixing Hector's airplane while he sleeps in the lounge. What did he bring to the job?"

"He's the manager," Wilbur said. He released the jack and stood up.

I still didn't let him off the hook. "Come on, Wilbur. What good has Hector done as manager?"

"Oh, I don't know," the little man said with a smile. "He hired you didn't he?"

27/ Frost Flying

The Pie area was good for farming. The growing season was extended by the "water bottle" effect of Lake Erie. This allowed Pie farmers to plant tobacco and other crops normally grown much further south. But sometimes the Canadian weather caught up with them. This usually happened on clear, calm, full moon nights in late April. Under those conditions, a temperature inversion occurred and a killer frost formed near the ground.

Since airplanes displaced air downward, it was logical to think they could push the warmer air above the crops down and prevent frost. This theory led to "frost flying." I had never heard of it. There came a time during my first spring at Pie In The Sky that I wished I still hadn't.

"You wanna frost fly?" Hector asked me one day.

"What's that?"

"It's flying over crops at first light on cold mornings to prevent frost from forming. Roger and I'll be doing it in the Pawnees, Leon and Frank will use school airplanes, but there'll be two left — one for you and a spare. It's usually for a few days in late April and early May. It's easy money."

I was interested. An opportunity to roar around on the deck like an ag pilot sounded like fun. After watching the aerial fertilizing, I had a secret longing to try it. This might be the next best thing. "I've never frost flown," I said.

"It's a cake walk. Sometime before the chance of frost, you drive over to the field in your car, meet the farmer and map out the obstacles. Then you fly a practice run over the farm in daylight. Start at 50 feet above the crop and work your way down to the deck. We've got several farmers on the waiting list. You could sign one up and give it a try."

I was sold. I thought an hour of low flying in the morning would be good for a change. I forgot that I was already working 12-hour days to finish off the college students who had been flying with Hector and Roger. I didn't know that "first light" in April came at 4:30 A.M.

The farmer on the top of the waiting list was a fruit grower. His property was too hilly for the mechanized tobacco farming, so he had planted apple, peach, and cherry trees. I called him and got directions to his farm. It was in a river gully, a rare break in the flat topography of the area. The house and barn sat in the middle of the farm at the end of a long lane. As I drove in, I could see that the obstructions above the fruit trees were the buildings, the hydro poles along the lane and the 50-metre ridges on both sides of the valley.

Miro Melinoski met me in the farmyard. He was young and keen. His whole broad face grinned while he worked my arm up and down with an overpowering handshake. He had rapid-fire speech that sounded like a tickertape machine with an accent. In the first two minutes of our meeting, I learned that Miro had been raised on a farm in Europe. When he finished school, he emigrated to Canada to work for a local tobacco grower. In seven years he had saved enough from his meager salary for a down payment on the abandoned farm in the valley. Miro was proud that he was successfully growing fruit in a tobacco area. He talked enthusiastically about hiring an aircraft for frost control.

"How do ve get dis togedder?" he asked excitedly.

"Well," I said, quoting from what Hector had told me, "if there is a chance of frost in the weather forecast, you set an alarm clock an hour before first light and go out and check a thermometer in your orchard. Try it in several places. On calm nights, the temperature can vary a lot over a small area. Do you have a thermometer?"

"Ya, ya," Miro said quickly.

"Good. If the temperature is near zero, give me a call at home. Let it ring several times. The charge for the callout and the first hour of flying is $150. If another hour is necessary, it's $100," I said.

At the time we were charging $24 an hour for a lesson in the Cessna 150, a loaf of bread was 25 cents and gasoline cost 40 cents — a gallon. I expected Miro to tell me to forget it.

"Ya, ya; goud, goud. I vill call," he sounded like I was doing him a favour.

"Here's my home phone number," I said, handing him a slip of paper. "I'm going to map out the obstructions now and do a test flight this afternoon. For that I charge you a $150 sign-up fee."

"Ya, goud, very goud."

"You should tell your neighbours what we're doing so they're not surprised by the low flying airplane," I said. There were several expensive-looking homes nestled in the valley.

"Don't vorry," Miro said, "ve don't bodder dem."

I sketched the farm showing the house, the wires and the ridges, and then drove back to the airport. From the air, the Melinosky farm looked different. Forty acres seemed a lot larger walking on the ground than from the air at 90 mph. I flew an initial pass at a polite 500 feet above the trees. It took me five seconds to cross the farm. I pulled into a climbing turn, heading for the ridge on the right side. I leveled off and turned left. The far ridge looked close. I increased the bank, pushed the rudder and headed down to the field. It wasn't pretty. I was flying the airplane like a student and was covering a lot of real estate. Even with the skidding steep turn, it was a full minute before I was over the orchard again. Ag flying was harder than it looked.

I was able to reduce the turn time by turning sooner, climbing less and banking steeper, but I was still too high. I'd have to go lower to do any good during a frost, but the idea bothered me. I'd spent my career teaching student pilots that altitude was money in the bank. I'd told them that low flying was dangerous, a nuisance to the ground-bound public and against the law.

So it seemed strange to push the Cessna 150 down. What if there were hydro wires that I had missed during my ground mapping? It felt like I was dangling my legs in a shark tank, but I inched lower on each pass. By the time I descended below 100 feet, I was starting to get comfortable with the pattern. I hadn't hit anything.

My initial fear gradually subsided and was replaced with exhilaration. Flying close to the ground was a lot of fun. Soon I was scooting near the tops of the fruit trees. It was a rush.

It also caught the attention of everyone in the valley. People on the ground pointed at me as I flew over. They must have wondered about an airplane dive-bombing an innocent orchard for an hour for no apparent reason.

I broke off the practice and headed for the airport. My arms and legs were sore from the constant turning, but I was grinning. In one flight, I had joined the ranks of agricultural pilots and it felt good.

I was anxious to try real frost flying. That night I checked the forecast before leaving the office. It called for a low of 12 degrees celcius. I went home disappointed. At three o'clock in the morning the phone rang. Susan answered it. My semi-conscious mind heard her say, "Get stuffed." She hung up.

I snapped awake. "Who was that?" I asked suddenly.

"Some crank foreigner wanted to know if I was frigid."

I realized it must have been Miro. A minute later the phone rang again. I answered it. "Hello?"

"Ello, dis is Miro. Are we frosty?"

"I don't know, Miro. What time is it?" I asked.

"Tree tirty."

"What's the outside temperature?"

"Ten degree," he said.

"Relax, Miro. That's not frosty enough." Now I was starting to talk like him. "Don't call me unless the temperature drops to three degrees, okay?"

"Okay, I vont."

At breakfast that morning, Susan asked me about the call. "Who was the guy on the phone last night?"

"That was Miro, the farmer I signed up for frost flying. Did he ask if you were frosty?"

"Yes. What's that all about?"

"I'm going to fly over his farm on cold mornings to mix the air up and hopefully prevent frost damage to the buds of his fruit trees."

"Why did he call in the middle of the night?" she asked.

"I don't know. I'm not supposed to fly until first light. It wasn't cold enough this morning, but he is anxious. Hopefully he won't call again until the temperature drops," I said.

"Do you know when first light is?" she asked. Her head was buried in the newspaper. She sounded annoyed.

"When the sun comes up," I replied with a laugh.

"Five oh-three this morning, according the paper. First light would be well before that," she said. "So Dracula is going to call every morning before four-thirty and ask if you're frosty?"

I must have paled visibly. I had been thinking of six o'clock. "Ah, just on the cold mornings," I replied. "Hector said it was only one or two days all year, only in the spring. The money is good," I added. "When I fly, I get paid triple my instructor salary per hour."

"And I'm going to get a wake-up call every time Dracula feels a chill?" she asked.

"Hopefully not too often," I replied.

"You can sleep on the other side of the bed," she said.

"Okay," I answered.

"With the phone ring turned down."

"I might not hear it," I said.

"Then sleep with your head on the night table," she said.

"Yes dear," I replied.

That afternoon's forecast called for a risk of frost in the low lying areas.

"Well, no drinking tonight," I announced to no one in particular in Wilbur's shop during lunch. "There's a frost warning."

"Speak for yourself," Hector said. "The farm I frost fly is not in a low lying area and the owner is cheap. He won't call until he can walk across the ice forming on his pond. By then it'll be too late, but I don't care. I'd rather sleep than save tobacco."

"Then I guess it's you and me for the dawn patrol, eh Roger?"

He smiled. "My farmer is Hector's farmer's brother. We've only flown them once in two years."

At 3:30 the next morning, the phone rang.

"Ello, I tink it's very frosty," Miro said. Susan was right, he did sound like Dracula.

"What's the temperature, Miro?"

"Tree. It's going down."

"All right, I'm on my way. Remember to wave me off if you don't need the second hour," I said. Secretly I hoped he needed several hours. If I was getting out of bed at 3:30, I wanted it to be worthwhile.

"Okay," he said.

I was the only one at the airport at 4:15. It was chilly, but I didn't see any frost in the dark. The moon was out, but it didn't offer much light.

I opened the hangar doors with the tractor and pulled out TWX. I did a quick walkaround inspection with a flashlight. The airplane's outside air temperature gauge read five degrees.

I thought I must be wasting my time and Miro's money, but I was there, so I decided to fly. A little warm air wasn't going to rob me of becoming a real frost pilot.

I took off at 4:30. It was still dark. Climbing out toward Miro's farm, I could see a tinge of light on the eastern horizon. It was warmer at 1,000 feet. I could feel the temperature change through the fresh air vents. The thermometer read 10 degrees.

I found the farm by the outline of the valley. The lights were on in Miro's house. It was too dark to see the trees, the wires or the ridges. The feeling of being a hotshot ag pilot melted away as I looked into the blackness below. I was either going to charge Miro for flying around his farm uselessly at 500 feet, or descend and kill myself.

I inched down to 300 feet during a series of long, slow, chicken passes. It was like flying in a vat of dark chocolate. I was still too high. If there was frost below, I wasn't doing any good. As the sky grew lighter, I got braver and flew lower. I could feel the temperature drop. The thermometer read minus two. I climbed back to the warmer air and tightened the pattern over the farm. Thirty minutes later I couldn't feel any temperature difference. I settled into a pattern of low passes connected by tight climbing turns.

At the end of an hour, the novelty of being a hot dog ag pilot was wearing thin. The exhilaration of low flying was turning into hard work. The repeated pattern was becoming routine. I would dive at the field, level off above the trees, pop over the wires, and dive back down over the trees. Then I'd pull up into a turn to repeat the pass in the other direction, moving over a little each time. The almost continuous turning and constant vigilance was wearing me out. I was beginning to wish Miro would wave me off. He didn't.

The daylight revealed the spectacle of several neighbours clad in PJs and parkas watching me from their porches. The police arrived. Two cars, one from each end of the valley, pulled into Miro's lane. Their flashing lights shone brightly in the pale light. I could see Miro gesturing to the policemen each time I skimmed by the house. One of the officers was writing on a note pad. They watched me for a while and left.

Toward the end of the second hour I didn't want to be an ag pilot any more. I wanted to be a sleepy-faced breakfast eater like the rest of the world. The sun was getting high in the sky and the air was warming up rapidly. Miro waved me off. It was 6:30. My first student was at 8:30 which left me enough time to scoot home for a quick breakfast and a shower.

Approaching the airport, I could see the flashing lights of a police car beside the office. I landed and parked at the gas pumps. The officer walked up to the airplane.

"Good morning sir," I said with a forced cheerfulness.

The older man was short, round and lumpy. He looked like a big potato in uniform. He wasn't very friendly. "Flyin' kind of low out there, weren't you?" he asked.

"Why do you ask?" I answered cautiously.

"I'm investigating a low flying complaint. Just answer yes or no," he said.

"No." I replied. I don't know why I chose denial, but it seemed like the right thing at the time.

"We'll let the judge decide," the surly officer said. "I need your name, address and I guess your pilot licence number."

While I was giving him the information, Hector arrived.

"Hi Dudley," Hector said to the cop, "What's up?"

"We gotta complaint about this here fella low flyin' over a house in the valley," Dudley said.

"So they sent Pie's finest out to investigate," Hector said. He sounded sarcastic.

"Huh?" Dudley asked.

I was about to step back into the conversation to prevent Hector from stretching my prison term into a life sentence, but he beat me to it. In a completely changed tone he said, "I'm glad to see you Dudley, it's been a long time since you've dropped by. Come on inside and we'll put some coffee on. It's uncivilized to stand out here this early in the morning."

Dudley wasn't smiling, but he liked the suggestion. "Yeah, good idea," he replied.

Hector unlocked the office door and I followed them in. I was nervous having to deal with the cop, but I was curious to see Hector in his new roll as a diplomat.

"You know," Hector said to Dudley as he was made coffee, "I'd be mad too if this character flew over my house at 5 o'clock in the morning. Didn't the farmer warn his neighbours that this would happen on frosty mornings?" Hector asked.

"I dunno," Dudley replied, "but we got a complaint and we gotta act on it."

"Of course, of course," Hector said. He filled a cup from the coffee maker and gave it to Dudley. "I'll let you do the fixings. I don't remember how you take it."

"Three sugar and two creams," Dudley replied.

"Same as me, help yourself. Now there must be some way we can convince this complainer that we are performing an essential service when we frost fly," Hector suggested.

"Yeah maybe, but buzzing somebody's house is illegal," Dudley said, testing the coffee.

"On the contrary," said Hector, handing me a coffee. "The law states that frost flying is allowed because of the good it does for the community."

This was a new one on me. Today there are separate air regulations governing agricultural flying which allow low level work, but in 1973 there were not. Ag pilots had to obey the same regs as airline pilots or anyone else. Now I was really curious. Hector was digging a big hole.

Dudley was curious too. "But there's a law that says no low flyin' over houses. We've been through this before," he said, looking perplexed.

"That's the one," Hector exclaimed, "That's the regulation that allows frost flying. I'll show you."

He went behind the counter to the bookshelf and after a little searching, pulled out a copy of the Department of Transport Air Regulations. It was quite dusty, but it didn't take him long to find what he wanted.

"Here it is," he said, carrying the binder over to Dudley. "It says that no one should fly below 1,000 feet above the highest obstacle in a built-up area unless they are not creating a hazard to persons or property on the ground. You see?" he said triumphantly. "Frost flying ELIMINATES a hazard to property on the ground. It's not only legal, it's necessary. Anyone trying to prevent frost flying would be obstructing the law."

Dudley scratched his head. "I'll have to check that one back at the station," he said, looking confused.

Hector jumped on the cop's hesitation.

"Before you do anything else, we'll go and talk to the guy. Maybe we can convince him to drop the complaint. That'll save you, him and us a lot of trouble. What do you say?"

Dudley hesitated. He obviously liked the "save you a lot of trouble" part of Hector's suggestion.

"Well, I dunno. I know this guy and he isn't easy to deal with," the policeman said nervously.

"Don't worry, we'll take care of it. Thanks Dudley, you're a good man," Hector said, putting his hand on the man's shoulder. "I'll send this wake-up ace over this morning and I'm sure everything will be all right."

"Well, okay," Dudley said, "But if the complaint stands, I'll have to come back."

"Sure, Dudley, I understand," Hector said. "Thanks, pal."

"Well, I'll be off," the cop said. "Thanks for the coffee."

"Anytime, Dud, it's always good to see you," Hector said, slapping him on the back. "Drop by anytime."

After the policeman left, Hector turned to me. He didn't have to say anything.

"I'm on my way," I said.

"Right," Hector replied.

I had to admit to myself that I was impressed by Hector's handling of the situation. It was a side of the often bumbling flying school manager that I had not seen before. I wasn't out of the woods yet, but I was in a much better position than before Hector had arrived.

Dudley had given us the name of the guy who had called the police. He was Miro's closest neighbour. I remembered the place from the air. It was a monstrous, new, H-shaped palace with a fountain in the middle of the cirular drive. There was an indoor swimming pool in the back half of the H. I drove up the long, red-stone driveway and parked by the fountain. I walked across the flagstone patio and knocked on the oak double doors. A portly older man answered. He was wearing a 1940s-style, double-breasted suit and was holding a large drinking glass. Bushy grey hair was growing out of his chin, his nose and his ears

— everywhere except the top of his head.

I introduced myself as the pilot who had woken him earlier.

"Pleased to meet you," he boomed, extending a beefy hand. "I'm Judge Theodore Hawthorne."

I accepted the handshake but almost fell over when he said, "Judge."

"Come in, my boy, come in," he said, motioning me into a cavernous front hall. Have a scotch?"

"Ah, no thanks, sir. It's early and I haven't had breakfast."

"My good man, scotch IS breakfast," he declared. He filled another tumbler with amber liquid from a decanter that was sitting on a sideboard by the front door. He handed me the glass and turned toward a sitting room. "Come in, come in. Now tell me what this is all about."

I sensed right away that it would be a mistake to try the Hector-style double-talk on the judge. I explained frost flying and apologized several times for bothering him. "Miro said there'd be no problems with his neighbours," I said, "so I assumed that he had talked to you."

"Miro would say that," the judge snorted. "Do you know where the word 'assume' comes from?" He didn't wait for an answer. "Make an ASS out of U and ME," he said, laughing at his own joke. "Miro is always trying something new, but he shoots first and asks questions later. Last time it was a new weed killer. It worked by over-fertilizing the weeds. They'd grow too fast and die. Miro sprayed it in a Force Seven gale. I had the largest daffodils in the world — for three hours, then they fell over and turned brown." He laughed as he recalled the incident. "But this frost flying sounds fascinating. Do you fly every morning?"

"Just when it's cold and there's a chance of frost," I said, sniffing my drink. My stomach said "No."

"So you might go tomorrow?" the judge asked.

"Yes sir, but if you'd rather I didn't, I'll tell Miro we can't do it."

"Nonsense, nonsense, I'd be glad to go. What time do we start?"

"At 4:30, sir."

"In the morning?"

"Yes, sir."

"Well then, so be it. If you're going tomorrow, give me a call and I'll meet you at the airport at 4:30."

It took a minute before I realized what he was suggesting. I played dumb, hoping I had heard him wrong. "Why do you want to meet me at the airport?" I asked.

"To go flying, of course. Why the hell else would I get up at 4:30 in the morning?"

"I see," I said tentatively. "It hadn't occurred to me that you'd be interested in riding along."

"I might as well if you're going to be buzzing around here like a flea in a mitt."

The mental image of the overweight, scotch-breathing judge stuffed into the Cessna 150 with me wasn't appealing. Worse was the thought of him wretching during two hours of hard flying. He'd probably change his mind when roused at 4:30, but just in case, I had to talk him out of it.

"I don't think you'd enjoy that kind of flying, especially that early in the morning — sir."

"Nonsense, nonsense. It'll be like a dawn patrol," he exclaimed. "Instead of hunting Huns, we'll hunt frost," he said with a belly laugh. "Here's to the call of the early morning," he said, raising his glass.

I raised mine, but while he was draining his, I said, "If you go flying, once we're airborne, you're committed. There's no turning back. We have to stay over the orchard until it warms up. It could take two hours of constant low level turning."

He plopped his empty tumbler on the table beside him. "You just want to have all the fun yourself," he declared with a grin and a burp. Then in a more serious tone, he added, "If you're going to fly low over a built-up area at 4:30 in the morning, the least you can do is take the old judge with you. To be candid, I don't think you have much choice."

With that, he stood up, signalling the end of our conversation. "I'll give you my phone number," he said.

"Yes sir," I replied. I followed him into the hall.

He wrote on a slip of paper and handed it to me. "I'll look forward to your call," he said.

"Yes sir, whatever you say."

During the drive back to the airport, I considered how to get out of frost flying with the judge. The forecast indicated there was a good chance of cold weather over the next several days. I could forget to call him, or call and let it ring only once and go without him. But the judge more or less had said take him or else. My concern went beyond the thought of being squished into the airplane with the pickled pontificator. It was possible the airplane wouldn't get off the ground with his extra weight and three hours of gas. I was also worried about seeing all that scotch come back when I started hauling the airplane around the orchard. I decided that my best hope was for him to change his mind when the time came.

When I returned to the flying school, Hector came into the office. "How did you make out?" he asked.

I told him about the judge. "The guy must weigh 250 pounds," I said, "I'm worried the airplane won't fly and if it does get off the ground, he'll probably puke in the first turn."

"It'll fly," Hector said, "but don't crank it around too much with that load. If it's any consolation, the two of you'll displace more air over the farm."

"Thanks a lot," I answered. Then I remembered seeing Hector fly 400 extra pounds of people in the Cessna 172 my first day at work. He probably knew what he was talking about.

"You're welcome," he said. "There's a frost warning for tonight, so you'll know soon enough."

I made it through the day despite the short night, no shower and little food. Near the end I was feeling numb, gummy and light headed.

Hector's forecast was accurate. Dracula called me at 3:30 the next morning. I was so tired I didn't hear it ring. Susan pounded me on the back to answer the phone.

"Ello, ve frosty," Miro said.

"Okay," I replied slowly.

I had about three seconds to stand up or fall asleep. I got out of bed, but couldn't feel my feet touching the floor.

The judge's number was beside the phone. It was the moment of reckoning. I dialed. It rang once and his voice boomed in my ear, "Squadron Operations, Wing Commander Hawthorne here — hee, hee."

"Good morning Judge, are you ready to pull some Gs?" I was hoping to scare him off.

"You bet, Ace. I wouldn't miss it for the world." He sounded genuinely excited.

"Okay, see you at the airport in 45 minutes," I said.

"Right, mission departure at oh four thirty; I'll be there."

He was waiting in his Lincoln when I arrived at the airport. "Good morning Captain," he said, climbing out of the car. "Are you ready to hunt frost?"

He was dressed in a one-piece, zippered-up jump suit and a baseball cap with gold leaves stitched on the peak. I think he was trying for the military look, but his bowling-pin shape wrecked the image. He was carrying a large thermos.

"Yes, Wing Commander," I replied. Playing along with his game made him giggle. I wondered if he and Johnny Walker had been up all night waiting for my call. His breath said "yes".

He helped me open the hangar doors and pull out TWX. "The Pie

Air Force really went overboard when it bought airplanes," he said sarcastically. He took a swig from the thermos.

"If you'd rather not go," I said quickly, "now is the time to speak up."

"No, no, the airplane is fine," he said, "but it looks like a single-seater. Where're you going to sit?"

"We both have to get in there," I replied.

I helped him into the right side of the Cessna and then squeezed into the other side. I had to hip-check him to make room to close my door.

"These frost fighters don't have much room, do they?" the judge said. He spoke so close to my face that I didn't have to guess what was in his thermos.

The Cessna did fly. It didn't exactly leap off the ground, but when I pulled back on the controls, the nose wheel lifted and the main wheels followed. The thicker, cool air probably helped.

The judge was animated.

"Up, up and away!" he shouted above the roar of the engine. "Give 'em hell."

My initial passes over Miro's farm were the same as the morning before — too high, too fast and useless against the frost. I might have been more daring without the judge, but it was still dark and the extra weight delayed the airplane's reaction to the controls.

After the third, long, gentle turn, the judge couldn't contain himself. "Is this it?" he asked. Is this what I got up at three A.M. for? When you were here yesterday, I saw some real flying. If I wanted a kiddy car ride, I'd go to the amusement park."

The outburst surprised me. I thought the combination of the early hour and high octane breakfast would have done him in, but apparently not. The sky was getting lighter. The dim outline of the tree tops appeared below. I dove for them, levelling off just high enough to clear the still invisible wires. We scooted across the farm and then I cranked the Cessna into a teardrop turn.

"Yahoo!" the judge yelled. "That's more like it! Go get 'um!"

I flew lower and tighter as the light improved and I got used to the heavy handling. I figured the judge would soon lose interest. I was wrong. He lost neither interest nor breakfast. The harder I flew, the happier he got. I stole a quick look at him when his enthusiastic shouting stopped in the middle of a turn. He was swigging from the thermos. I opened my fresh air vent to escape the whiskey fumes.

"Drink?" he yelled, stuffing the container in my face.

"No thanks," I yelled back, trying to concentrate on hopping the wires.

As the gravity force switched from positive to negative to positive over the wires, the judge expertly moved his thermos up and down to keep the contents inside. "Ride 'um cowboy," he shouted. "Give 'em hell."

I settled into a steady rhythm of low passes connected by tight turns. The longer I manoeuvered, the more the judge liked it. "This is great," he said as I stood the Cessna on a wing. "Just like the French countryside in the spring of '43. This is no Mosquito, but the altitude is right for a morning strafing sortie."

"You flew in the war?" I asked. I had difficulty imagining the judge as a fighter pilot.

"I sure did. It was a lot of years and a lot of pounds ago, but I parted a few fruit trees in my time."

"No wonder you're enjoying this," I said.

"You bet," he declared. "Can I try it?"

"NO!" I said instantly, but it didn't do any good. The judge grabbed the other control wheel as we were skimming the tops of the trees. When we passed the end of Miro's farm, he snapped the airplane into a climbing turn. "Piece of cake," he declared loudly.

My hand stayed on the control wheel anticipating the worst. I hoped to overpower him if necessary, but it wasn't. The judge's flying wasn't perfect, but with a few extra corrections, he flew us over the field as well as I could. After a couple of passes, I started to relax. The judge was quiet for a change, concentrating on his flying.

He flew for 20 minutes. "You got it, he said, lifting his hands as we darted past the second floor of Miro's house. "I'm getting tired."

I took control. The judge drank from his thermos and then fell asleep. He didn't wake up until I cut the power on landing after a two-hour flight. As soon as we came to a stop on the ramp, he struggled out of the Cessna and waddled off to the office washroom to relieve his liquid breakfast.

He came back out while I was refueling the airplane and shook my hand. "I want to thank you for letting me go along and relive some old memories," he said.

"You're welcome, Judge," I said. It was a genuine reply. "Although I'll remind you that you didn't give me much choice."

"I guess you're right," he said with a smile. "Well, don't call me tomorrow. I've had my fun and I know I'll be able to sleep through anything now. Thanks again."

The judge never flew with me again, although he had plenty of opportunities. The spring of '73 had a record number of cold mornings. By the beginning of May the dark circles under my eyes covered my whole face and I could almost fly over Miro's farm in my sleep. The extra income was good at first, but soon I had to cancel students in the afternoon to make it through the day.

The frost flying became monotonous except for one bright spot. When it was light enough to see the ground, I could often spot the judge sitting in a lawn chair under the glass enclosure of his swimming pool, saluting me with a glass of scotch as I flew over.

28/ Bombs Away

Wilbur checked out Hector in one of the Avengers. Originally the torpedo bombers had three seats — pilot, navigator and turret gunner. The crew sat one behind the other under a greenhouse-style canopy. In the Pie airplanes the seats, guns and panels had been removed from the two back positions to save weight.

For his checkout, Hector stood in the navigator's space behind Wilbur. He watched him fly for an hour, doing mostly takeoffs and landings. Then Wilbur put Hector in the pilot's seat and stood on the wing for a dry run of procedures while parked on the ramp. After another hour, he patted Hector's helmet and jumped off.

Wilbur walked over to where I was refueling a Cessna. "Don't you go with him on his first flight?" I asked.

"No, sir," he said without hesitation. "If he needs help, I don't want to be there. There's no dual controls. If I went with him, all I could do was scream. I'd rather do that here."

We watched while Hector performed the cockpit dance that all radial engine pilots do when starting up. The primer, starter, throttle, mixture and ignition all had to be adjusted at the same time. It sounds impossible and nearly is, but after a few turns of the prop, Hector was rewarded with a "cough, pop and a burp," followed by the irregular staccato of all nine cylinders firing. Soon the 1,900-horsepower engine settled into a deep-throated rumble. Hector released the brakes and gave us a "thumbs up" as he taxied out. His grin barely fit in the cockpit.

I walked back into the office to see if my next student had arrived. By the time I was inside, Hector was starting his takeoff. The constant speed propeller was set for maximum rpm. The noise thrown by the big blades was incredible as the tips went supersonic. This was normal, but Hector was slow to reduce the rpm after takeoff. I imagined he was busy making sure he did everything else right first — flaps up, gear up, trim set, power back, watch the speed, and then rpm decrease. The houses off the end of runway 09 got to hear all horses at full power.

The phone rang. I answered it. "I'm sorry I can't hear you," I said to the lady on the other end of the line. "There's too much noise in the backgr...." I recognized the noise. It was Hector's propellor tips. It sounded like they were in the lady's kitchen.

"THAT'S WHY I'M CALLING," she yelled. "MY DISHES ARE JUMPING OFF THE SHELVES!"

I could hear the china rattle over the phone. It must have been Mrs. Shaw, the widow who lived across the street from the end of runway 09. She often called during an Avenger takeoff. The propeller noise on the phone receeded. "Thank you for calling. It's always nice to hear from our neighbours," I said.

"Don't try and butter me, sonny," she growled. "I've lived here long enough to know you two-faced flyers and I'm telling you I don't have to listen to that kind of noise. You tell that pilot that if my dishes so much as click on his next takeoff, I'm going to call the Department of Transport and make sure he spends the rest of his career flying a bus."

"Yes ma'am," I said. "I...." She hung up.

I asked Susan to call Hector on the unicom and tell him to avoid Mrs. Shaw. Then I went flying with my student. When we returned, Hector's Avenger was parked beside the terminal building. The garden hose was filling the hopper. The next part of his checkout was to practise spraying the triangular piece of land between the runways with water.

Hector was drinking coffee in the office. "Susan told me old Mrs. Shaw called," he said with a laugh. "She calls every year. As soon as the first Avenger takes off, you can bet the old biddy will be on the phone."

"She sounded pretty upset," I said.

"She's upset every year," he replied.

"Well, don't worry," I said. "she won't call here again. Next time she's going to phone the Department of Transport. She has your licence number written on her kitchen wall."

He looked at me sideways. He didn't know if I was kidding.

"Seriously," I said, "you should back off the power flying over her place."

"Sure, boss," he replied.

I was walking out to a Cessna 150 with a student when Hector took off for his spray practise. The wind dictated that he depart eastbound again. The noise of the snarling radial engine echoed off the side of the hangar as he accelerated. With the load of water he used more runway. As soon as he was airborne, Hector reduced the power. The airplane hesitated in the climbout.

I was about to turn away when I saw the bottom of the hopper open. The Avenger's entire load dropped in one 4,000-pound pillar of water. The silvery glob fell on the Shaw house. Hector had pulled the emergency dump handle instead of the landing gear lever. The Avenger shot up, having rid itself of the weight. Hector circled for a landing.

I trotted back into the office expecting to hear the phone ring. It already had. Susan was holding the receiver away from her ear. I could hear Mrs. Shaw yelling from across the room. Susan waved me off so I left her to handle the old lady and headed back outside. Hector was taxiing in. When he had shut down, I walked over. "The water you dumped hit Mrs. Shaw's house," I called up to him.

"Hee, hee, that'll fix the old girl," he laughed.

"You'd better go see her and smooth things over. Susan is listening to her rant on the phone right now."

"Okay, boss."

I went flying. At the end of the lesson I flew over the Shaw's house. It was ringed with emergency vehicles. After screaming at Susan, the old lady had phoned the local police, the fire department, the ambulance service, the newspaper, Pie radio station and every member of the town council, including the mayor.

I landed, finished with my student and drove over to the scene. From the road, the house looked normal except for the jam of assorted vehicles. The back was a different story. The water had hit the yard and the rear of the house. It had ripped out Mrs. Shaw's prize rose bushes and propelled them through her sliding glass doors into the living room along with her cast iron lawn furniture. All the windows on that side of the house were blown in and the shingles were stripped off the back of the roof. The rear half of the house had been destroyed.

The old lady was not hurt. She had been in a front bedroom when the water hit. She was complaining to anyone who would listen. "They did it on purpose," she wailed to a reporter. "They've been trying to force me out for years."

Hector was talking to Dudley, the policeman, who was writing in his notebook. The rest of the emergency crews were leaving. I heard one of the firefighters comment, "It looks like we've already been here."

That's nearly the end of the incident. The air service's insurance company paid for the repairs. The Department of Transport reviewed the police report and decided further action was unnecessary. Hector completed his training without causing any more damage. The coverage in the Pie Plain Dealer gave Mrs. Shaw the last word on the incident, "They think they'll scare me into moving, but they haven't seen the last of me yet."

She was right.

29/ Tower of Shaw

When Mrs. Shaw was having her house rebuilt, she ordered the contractor to replace her TV antenna with a 50-foot tower. It was her way of retaliating for Hector's bombing.

The Shaw house was across the road from the end of the runway, so the obstruction was not much of a hazard. In fact, we used it to teach takeoffs and landings over an obstacle. If there was any doubt the student would clear the antenna, we flew around it. The tower was a Hangar Club conversation piece and a local aviator's landmark. It didn't cause a problem until the airport inspector came around.

Once a year a Department of Transport official visited Pie Airport to see if it continued to meet the minimum government specifications for a licenced airport. Asphalt conditions were checked, along with pavement markings, the distance of new buildings from the runways and new obstructions.

Clay Gorman met with the inspector. Clay was the Pie Parks and Recreation worker who arranged for the airport snow plowing in winter and grass cutting in the summer. Clay was an "everybody's uncle" kind of guy — round and friendly, and permanently locked into a municipal worker's slow pace.

"How far is that tower from the runway?" the inspector asked him.

"I don't know," Clay said.

"How high is it?"

"About that high," Clay said, grinning and holding his thumb and forefinger up to the tower in the distance. He was supposed to know what went on around the airport, but 30 years as a city employee had taught Clay to know as little as possible.

"I'm going to have to check it out," the inspector said.

"You go ahead," Clay said, "I'll wait for you in the lounge. Mrs. Shaw owns that house and she eats city officials for breakfast."

The inspector drove around to visit Mrs. Shaw. When the old lady found out who he represented, she invited him in, made tea and filled his ears about the trials of living near an airport inhabited by renegade pilots. When he finally returned, he had bad news.

"The tower cuts through the night approach slope requirements for runway 27. There can't be any obstruction above a 1:14 angle off the end of any runway used at night."

"That's the only runway with lights," Clay said.

"Well, if you don't want to install lights on another runway, the other choice is to displace the night threshold of runway 27 seven hundred feet. Then the approach clears the required slope."

"That leaves only 1,800 feet," Clay said.

"It's that or nothing. You tell me what you're going to do and I'll issue a Notice to Airmen explaining the change."

"Okay, I'll displace the threshold for now."

Clay went out and unscrewed the first seven bulbs on each side of runway 27. The inspector drafted a NOTAM about the change and told Clay to send an amendment to the government map office responsible for printing the Chart Supplement of airport information for pilots. Clay posted a notice on the flying school bulletin board.

"I suppose we could add short field landings to the night rating course," Jethro said.

"Now you're talking like a true enterprising civilian," I said.

The displaced threshold was a joke until Bob and Tom flew in with the King Air. "You saving electricity or what?" Bob asked me when he read the notice.

"No, its the new TV tower on the approach that's forcing the displaced threshold," I replied.

"That's too bad 'cause we can't do 1,800 feet at night with the King Air. The boss will be mad when I tell him Pie is now a daylight only operation."

I phoned Clay right away and told him the problem. I discovered there is nothing that will move city officials better than an industry nervous about its location. Clay asked the city treasurer if the airport budget would cover lights for another runway.

"Not in your lifetime," was the reply.

He asked the city legal counsel if they could force Mrs. Shaw to remove the tower.

"I'll look into it," he said.

That same day the lawyer called Clay into his office and told him there was a mechanism to solve the problem. "When the City of Pie took over the airport from the federal government," the lawyer said, "the town council passed a by-law prohibiting structures that infringed on the airport's operation. Once you file a protest with Bruce Appleby, the By-Law Enforcement Officer, he can see Judge Hawthorne for an in-

125

junction. Once he serves that on the property owner, she'll have to remove the tower or we'll do it for her."

Clay went to Bruce Appleby. "According to my records, Mrs. Shaw doesn't own the house," Bruce told him. "Her son does."

"Can you serve the injunction on him?" Clay asked.

"I've looked into that already. I could, but he's in the army, serving in Cypress."

"Oh."

The next day Clay told us the whole story over coffee in Wilbur's shop. "Shaw's son won't be back for six months," he said.

"So we're stuck with the displaced threshold until then?" I asked.

"I'm afraid so. I can't think of any other way around it."

Leon, one of the Avenger pilots, was listening. He was waiting for his hopper to fill with water so he could fly a practice spray run.

"Well, something should be done," Leon declared. Then he got up, rinsed his cup and ambled out to the ramp.

The rest of us went back to work. I heard Leon start the Avenger while I was briefing my first student. The big spray plane taxied out for takeoff while we were walking out to the flight line. We stopped our walkaround inspection on the Cessna 150 to watch Leon take off from runway 27. He flew a circuit and lined up for a landing. The wheels were down, the speed was down and the power was up. He was low. At the last minute Leon cocked the Avenger into a sideslip. He lined up his left main wheel with Mrs. Shaw's new TV tower and neatly slammed it to the ground. There was no fuss, no bother and no contest. The aluminum tower was no match for the Avenger.

My student's eyes popped when he realized what he was watching. "Wow, it looked like he did that on purpose," he said.

"Yup, it sure did."

30/ Blast Off

The combined roar of 7,600 horsepower vibrated my chest. It sounded great. The source was the Pie's four Avengers departing for New Brunswick. They taxied out together with Wilbur in the lead aircraft. The spray contract was for three aircraft. The fourth was a spare that Wilbur had loaded with tools and parts. He would be staying in New Brunswick to do the maintenance on the Avengers. The little, old mechanic looked funny perched on four cushions in the big airplane. He had to weave back and forth on the taxiway to see over the nose. Frank, Leon and Hector followed in the other aircraft.

I stood by the office door and watched them perform a loose formation takeoff from runway 09. They flew straight over Mrs. Shaw's house. The old lady had remained strangely silent when Leon dropped her TV tower the day before.

Susan yelled to me across the lounge over the dying roar of the departing Avengers, "It's Mrs. Shaw on the phone."

"Yes, Mrs. Shaw, I hear them," I bellowed over the engine noise coming through her phone. "Someone should have warned you they were departing. I'm sorry." It was hard to sound apologetic when yelling so loud. The noise subsided. "Well, at least they're gone for the season, Mrs. Shaw. They won't be back for a long time. I'm sorry for the inconvenience. Thanks for calling."

I was sorry to see them go. I knew I'd miss the comraderie of the Hangar Club in Wilbur's shop. More important, their departure signalled a drop in activity at the flying school. Jethro and I had been busy finishing off the Private Pilot courses of the college students and farmers who had flown all winter, but we weren't getting new customers to replace them like we had earlier in the year.

It wasn't for a lack of trying. I ran ads in the local paper offering $5 introductory flights. Susan and I produced a newsletter and sent it to our customers promoting advanced ground schools and fly-ins to other airports. The result was unanimous — no new students and a steady decline in activity of our current customers. After watching Hector stumble his way to profit through the winter, it was discouraging to see the balance sheet tip the other way.

As our income dropped, our costs went up. This was the first year the Middle East countries flexed their oil muscles by raising prices. The cost of aviation fuel had increased from 39 cents to 52 cents an imperial gallon in less than 12 months.

Our maintenance costs also went up. Wilbur arranged for Stefan Wolaski from London, Ontario to work on Roger's Pawnee and the school aircraft on an on-call basis. It was expensive because we had to pay him travelling money and the cost wasn't spread over as many airplanes.

These worries were running through my head as I watched the Avenger formation circle the airport at low altitude. I didn't know until then that a Pie In The Sky major departure always included a beat-up of the airport. The four torpedo bombers came directly over the office. This time Susan and I were treated to all the noise and rattling fury of the formation at full speed. Everything loose in the office, including the furniture, started "walking" with the vibration.

"Why do they do that?" Susan asked.

"I guess it's just for fun," I said, watching them cross the field. "It doesn't hurt anything over the airpor...."

I didn't finish the sentence because I realized they were headed straight for Mrs. Shaw's house, still at full speed, still on the deck. The phone rang.

"I'll get it," I said. "I know who it is."

31/ In Tight

"Here, hold this," Roger said, handing me the end of a tape measure.

"Okay," I replied. I didn't have a clue what he was up to. I had stuck my head out of the office after seeing him lay the tape on the ground by the front door.

"Put that against the steps," he directed.

I did. Roger walked toward the flag pole at the edge of the parking lot, reeling off the tape as he went.

"Just as I thought," he declared with satisfaction.

"What are you doing?" I asked.

"Measuring the distance between the office and the flag pole," the big pilot replied calmly.

"I can see that," I said. "Are you going to tell me why?"

"Sure, but first, come and help me measure the other side." He headed around the building.

I followed him to the airside of the office.

"Hold this against the door," he said.

Roger then measured the distance from the door to the light standard next to the ramp.

"Clay asked me to fertilize the lawn if I had any nitrogen left over. I want to make sure it'll fit."

"What will fit?" I asked. I still hadn't caught on.

"The Pawnee," he replied.

"You're going to fly the Pawnee between the building and the light standard?" I asked. The distance didn't look wide enough for a Pitts Special.

"I am, now that I know it'll fit," Roger replied.

"It will?"

"Yup. Forty feet; I only need thirty-six."

"You're crazy," I declared. The big pilot smiled in agreement.

I looked around. The flag pole and light standard were not Roger's biggest obstacles. The hangar stood three stories high not far from the office.

"Ah, Roger. What about the hangar?"

"No problem," Roger replied.

"You're really crazy."

Later that day Roger fertilized the lawn. I was in the office when he did it. I heard him coming and looked up to see the Pawnee heading straight for the building. He was in level flight doing about 80 mph. The airplane's main wheels were almost touching the ground.

It looked like he was going to crash into the office. At the last second, he rolled the Pawnee into a lazy right turn and flashed by the front window. He was so close I could see the rib stitching in the fabric under the left wing. The turn carried Roger between the light standard and the terminal building. He continued to roll close to a vertical bank. The Pawnee didn't go over the hangar, it went around, pivoting on its right wing. It was close. I could feel goose bumps rising on my skin as I watched.

Roger stayed low, flying between the aircraft on the ramp and rolling left to circle the hangar. I went to the front to watch him fly inside the flag pole. This time he came from the hangar side. He started his fertilizing run in a vertical bank and rolled out of it as he passed me. I had opened the door. Roger was so close that tiny nitrogen pellets rolled across the floor inside.

It was beautiful and scary at the same time. He did two more passes, one front and one back, this time flying in the opposite direction, just to prove his clean runs were not flukes.

Susan didn't know enough to be impressed. "Why is he flying so close to the building?"

"To fertilize the lawn."

"Oh."

Clay's reaction was the best. The city worker had been outside digging in the flower bed when Roger flew over. He came into the office and stood there wide-eyed and grinning. There were nitrogen beads stuck in his thinning hair. "Oohee! Did ya see that? I thought I was done for sure. Vrroomm," Clay made his hand swoop to imitate the Pawnee. "Then he came back and did it again. I darn near wet myself. I couldn't believe it."

Clay noticed the nitrogen on the floor. "Say, that airplane sure makes quick work of fertilizing. Do ya suppose Roger would do the lawn around City Hall?" he asked.

After seeing this display, I figured Roger could and would do anything. "Yes, I'm sure he would," I said. "but do him a favour, don't ask."

"Sure, okay," he replied.

32/ Emmy-Lou

A colourful mixed bag of privately-owned aircraft were tied down at the Pie Airport. Emmy-Lou was my favourite. Emmy-Lou was the name of an Aeronca Chief belonging to Tim O'Connell, a young computer technician from northern Ontario. Tim was a likeable guy who carried a zest for life and the self-assurance to go with it. He had moved to the area the previous fall, bringing the family airplane with him.

During the winter Tim didn't fly the Chief, but he visited the airport regularly to sweep the snow off his airplane and chat. One day over coffee he told me his dad had "acquired" the Chief in exchange for an old pickup truck, and two heifers. "The calves came from good stock," he said with a smile.

I believed him. I knew nothing about cows, but the Chief was obviously a two-heifer airplane. It had seen better days. Aeronca had built the Chief in the 1940s when all small airplanes were fabric covered, lightweight and slow. On Tim's, the fabric was faded and sagging, oil streaks traced the curve of the airflow along the sides of the fuselage. The airplane looked a little sad sitting lopsided in its tie-down.

"We call her Emmy-Lou," Tim said.

"Emmy-Lou?" I asked.

"We named the airplane after the two calves," he explained.

"Oh," I said.

"She's fun to fly," he continued without being asked, "but she's got no heater, so I don't go up much this time of year."

I nodded in agreement. The little airplane had a large wing and I imagined free-spirited Tim riding her lazily through the air on a warm summer day enjoying a great slow view of the countryside. But I was secretly glad that I didn't have to fly the airplane. The school's new, all-metal Cessnas had spoiled me. I had flown in the bush. I'd had enough of drafty, smelly, slow airplanes.

On the first nice weekend of the spring, Tim brought his girlfriend to the Pie Airport. They parked beside the Chief, turned up the car radio, pulled out an array of cleaning supplies and attacked the winter grime on Emmy-Lou. Their work was interspersed with frequent water fights and coffee breaks. It was a scene I liked to see. It represented the ideal in the sport of flying. Too many people dropped out of aviation after receiving their licence. Most new pilots rented the flying school airplanes to take friends and relatives for rides, but not many kept it up and almost none bought aircraft. Tim was a guy who had. Emmy-Lou wasn't much of an airplane, but Tim was enjoying her.

I watched Tim and Jean (he had introduced her to Susan and I in the lounge) pull the airplane from the tie-down. Jean climbed into the right seat and Tim hand-started the engine by flipping the propeller. Then he squeezed into the left side. The little airplane looked much happier clean. The fabric still sagged, but the oil streaks and winter grime were gone. When they taxied out for takeoff, the Chief dogtracked on its lopsided landing gear, but it looked eager to fly.

I was busy with students and didn't think of the pair until I returned from my last flight. The Chief was back in its spot. Tim and Jean were relaxing in the lounge and talking to Susan behind the desk.

"Did you have a good flight?" I asked. I looked at Jean to gauge her reaction to an afternoon of bouncing around in the warm spring air. Susan in the same situation would have been slumped in a chair with clenched teeth, concentrating on her stomach, but Jean appeared bright-eyed and cheerful.

"Great," was Tim's enthusiastic response, "It was super to get back up there."

Jean smiled in agreement.

"I felt a little rusty, though," Tim continued.

"Well, that's normal," I replied, "You haven't flown all winter. Did you find the old skill came back quickly?"

"Oh yeah," Tim said, leaning on the counter, "but I was thinking I should take some lessons."

It was not unusual for aircraft owners to ask instructors to fly with them occasionally. Their insurance companies often required an annual review of emergency procedures and general flying ability. It was probably okay to drift around in Tim's old Chief on a sunny Saturday, but I wasn't keen on exploring the flight envelope in it. That might be asking too much of the old fabric and tubes. Besides, Tim probably knew more about flying the Chief than I did.

"So you want me to shoot a few landings with you?" I asked, hoping that's all he needed.

"Yeah, whatever it takes to get a licence."

The colour drained from my face. "You don't have a pilot licence?" I asked in a rising voice.

"Nope," he said casually. "I flew with my neighbour, Mert, for a few minutes when we bought the airplane. He showed me some things, but he wasn't very good. I did much better on my own."

I took a deep breath. A rush of thoughts flooded my mind. The first was disbelief, but I knew Tim well enough to know this was no joke.

"How long ago?" I asked.

"Two years," he replied.

I wondered how he had stayed alive. It must have been a scary two years. At the time, students at the flying school were averaging 12-15 hours of instruction before doing a first solo takeoff and landing, and 40 hours before receiving a pilot licence. It didn't seem possible for someone to teach himself to fly.

My next concern was the Chief's mechanical condition. It probably wasn't good. If Tim had been flying with no licence, I would have bet it was ditto for the airplane. Now he wanted me to fly with him.

These thoughts were interrupted by the polite stares of Tim and Jean. They were waiting for me to speak.

"Well, I agree, lessons would be a good idea." I said cheerfully. There was no sense lecturing and embarrassing Tim in front of his girl-friend. "Let's book some time now," I said.

"Sure, weekends are best for me," he replied.

"Okay, next Saturday then."

We set a time and then Tim asked me how long the lessons would take.

"Well, the minimum dual flight instruction for a Private Pilot Licence is 12 hours," I said. "then you take a flight test. There is also a written exam. Are you available for our ground school on Monday nights?"

"Sure, I could be," he said easily.

"One other thing," I said.

"Yes?"

"Has the aircraft been inspected by a mechanic for an annual Airworthiness Certificate?"

"No, it runs fine," he said, looking puzzled. "I've never had it in a shop."

"Well, it's a government requirement to have an airplane inspected by a certified mechanic at least once a year. Would you mind if I let Stefan take a look at it this week?"

I didn't say that I wouldn't fly with him if the answer was "no" and I didn't tell him what kind of trouble he would be in if the government discovered what he was doing. Not yet.

"No problem," he said, a little less cheerfully, "I'd appreciate a call if he finds anything major."

"Sure, of course," I said.

"Anything else?" he asked, reading the expectant look on my face.

"Just one," I said, relieved he had asked. "Do you happen to have insurance on the aircraft?"

"No, my Dad always said, 'If you break your toys, then you fix 'em or do without.' Is it a problem?"

"No, but I'll get you to sign a waiver before we go up. It says you won't hold me responsible if we wreck your airplane and it's my fault."

"Sure, no problem."

I honestly expected Stefan to end Tim's flying. I figured he would condemn the airplane's fabric or the engine, or both. Either would have required repairs well beyond the value of the aircraft.

I misjudged Stefan's rural approach to airworthiness. That Monday he came into the office to deliver the verdict on Emmy-Lou's condition. "She's fine," he declared.

I waited. He didn't offer any more details. "Fabric's fine?" I asked.

"Yup."

"What about the sags?"

"Sags are fine," he answered.

"Stefan, airplane covering is not supposed to sag."

He drew a deep breath, and let it out slowly, giving me one of his looks. "Dere's no damage underneath," he said. "Steel tubing is sound and rust free. Fabric is sagging because it vasn't put on right. Dat may be a problem at high Mach, but in dat airplane I don't think ve vorry about sound barrier."

"How about the oil leaks?" I asked.

"Fixed. I replaced rocker cover gaskets."

"Compression?"

"Vhat compression?"

"The engine compression, how was it?"

"Dat's vhat I said, vhat compression? Dat's a 65-horsepower engine. You get enough power to turn propeller and dat's all. Dere's no afterburner." Stefan sounded impatient, but I knew he enjoyed lecturing pilots. "It's an airplane to fly, not drive. It'll be good for you. I fixed landing gear so both sides of the airplane vork together."

That was it. The airplane had passed and I was condemned to fly it. As much as I hated to admit it, Pie In The Sky needed the business. Tim was our first new student in a month. Instructing him in his own aircraft did not provide much income for the school, but it kept me busy.

On the first lesson, I followed Tim around during his pre-flight inspection. It gave me a chance to see the Chief close up. It was an education. Tim showed me how he checked the engine oil level and drained a sample of gas from the little bowl under the fuel tank in the nose. That was it. He stood there smiling.

I frowned. "There's much more to look for," I said. "Let's start at the nose and I'll show you a complete inspection. First, check the propeller for knicks," I said, looking at Tim and running my hand along the leading edge of the prop. I stopped. I had flown aluminum propellers. They were sometimes chipped by little stones and debris on the runway. The Chief's prop was wooden. I was feeling the solid brass covering on its leading edge. It would have taken a collision with an iron bridge to knick it.

"Seems fine," I said and continued. "When you're checking the oil, take a minute to look at the rest of the engine. You may find fuel or oil leaks, or a bird's nest." Stefan had sprayed Tim's engine with varsol. It was perfectly clean. Tim nodded politely.

"Check the tires for knicks, cuts and tread," I said, bending over the right wheel. There were none — no knicks, no cuts and no tread. The fat little tires were as smooth as an eight ball. I looked at Tim. He was still smiling politely. "Maybe we could talk to Stefan about new tires sometime," I said. "We need tread for grip during crosswind takeoffs and landings, especially in the rain."

"They came like that," was all Tim said. He left it for me to determine how he had survived flying for two years on no tread.

"Check the windows," I said turning to the cabin. I stopped again. The windshield wasn't bad, just crazed in the corners, but the plastic side windows were milky. It was difficult to see through them.

"Maybe we can talk to Stefan about new plexiglass in the side windows," I said.

"I fly with them open," Tim replied.

No wonder he didn't fly in the winter.

Part of the Chief's control cables ran outside the fabric. I showed Tim how to check their connections. "Give the cables a shake. You can tell if they're tight," I said, jiggling a rudder cable. "These are a bit stretched," I declared, hearing the cable slap the fabric where it ran inside the fuselage. "The controls will be less responsive, but we can still fly. I'll talk to Stefan after." Tim gave me a quizzical look, but again nodded politely.

"Then have a general look at the fabric," I said, running my hands over the wrinkles. We had discussed these after my lecture from Stefan.

"Check for holes and tears," I continued. There were none.

I stood there looking at Emmy-Lou. There was nothing else to check. I found the pitot tube sensor for the airspeed indicator, and showed Tim how to check it was not clogged. But there were no other fuel drains, no static sensors for the altimeter, no alternator belt, no lights, no radio antennas, no flaps, and no air vents.

"Well, I guess that's it," I said. "Let's go flying."

I climbed into the right seat. Tim showed me how to hold the brakes while he hand-propped the engine. It started first try.

The Chief's side-by-side seating was a tight squeeze for two guys. Sliding the windows open gave us more shoulder room. The instrument panel was stark. There were no radios, no switches and no circuit breakers, just dials for airspeed and altitude, a compass and an oil pressure gauge. A curved carpenter's level served as a slip indicator.

Tim taxied to the runway. My plan was to let him fly and watch his homebrewed methods to see what needed "unteaching." I hoped he wouldn't quit when we went beyond the 12-hour minimum.

The name Emmy-Lou was appropriate for the Chief. The airplane was nice, but slow and simple. Tim ran up the engine beside the runway and checked each half of the dual ignition. There wasn't much else to do before takeoff. Tim checked seat belts, doors closed, gas on, trim set, and controls free.

He looked around for other traffic and pulled onto the runway. When he applied full power, the onslaught of noise announced great things that never came. The main product of the Chief's engine was sound. The airplane wobbled slowly down the runway like a constipated duck.

The actual liftoff caught me by surprise. There was no fuss or bother, the Chief just floated into the air at an impossibly slow speed, its pithy motor struggling to make a breeze. The ground dropped away in slow motion.

Tim turned toward the practice area near the lakeshore. He didn't know it, but I was using the turn as his first big test. In old, slow airplanes, turns are difficult to coordinate properly. Applying aileron control produces a bank, but no change in direction, the airplane slumps over on its side and continues straight ahead. The correction is to add rudder control with the ailerons. In modern airplanes, the problem is compensated by the way the ailerons are hinged.

The turn was perfect. I asked him do a few more to make sure. Each one was as good as the first.

"Who taught you to apply rudder into the turns?" I yelled over the full throttle engine noise?

Tim looked blank and shrugged. He didn't know what I was talking about. Apparently he had experimented with the controls until he found the right combination. Tim was sharp enough and the Chief was slow enough that he had taught himself.

In one hour, Tim demonstrated proficiency in most of the Private Pilot's course. I learned more than he did. I discovered that the Chief was stuck in slow flight. The airspeed indicator never moved over 65 mph, even in a dive. I learned that sloppy control cables do not affect an airplane that offers only a grudging response at the best of times. I learned that in a glide a Chief will climb in a thermal. Approaching the runway into the light breeze, Tim landed the lightweight airplane with little forward ground speed. The bald tires barely turned.

I learned to like the Chief. The airplane grew on me like an old chair. Emmy-Lou was a go-nowhere-in-a-hurry, fun airplane to fly.

My next problem was deciding what to do with Tim for 11 more hours. The cross-country helped. The standard Pie In The Sky dual navigation lesson was a two-hour, triangular flight to Sarnia and then Stratford, Ontario. It took us four and a half. I thought the cross-country would be my first chance to actually teach Tim something. I knew from his confessions in the ground school classes that he had been navigating by following roads. He had never used a circular computer for speed, time and fuel calculations. During the briefing before the cross-country flight, he obediently marked our course on his map and circled the major landmarks every ten miles for ground speed checks.

We took off from runway 09 and turned on course. It was a clear day, so I made Tim level off at 500 feet to make the trip more challenging. We crossed the airport boundary. "Sixty," Tim shouted over the engine noise.

"Sixty what?" I shouted back.

"Ground speed is sixty miles per hour," he declared, "We'll be there in one hour. Fuel burn will be three gallons."

"How do you know?" I asked. We hadn't reached the first landmark.

"The runway is half a mile long, right?"

"Yes."

"It took us 30 seconds to fly it. That's a mile a minute. Fuel burn is always three gallons an hour. That's half a gallon every ten minutes. I don't need a computer for the rest." He was grinning.

"Use the computer anyway," I replied, "just to make me happy."

Tim had no trouble map reading at that speed on a clear day. At the first checkpoint, he recalculated the speed, time and fuel using the computer. The figures didn't change.

We spent the rest of the trip sightseeing low to the ground. We waved at farmers, chased hawks and raced a few cars (and lost). We also talked ourselves hoarse. I discovered that Tim was a down-to-earth, knowledgeable and friendly guy.

Over the next two weeks we burned off the remaining minimum hours with spins. It was the only manoeuver Tim hadn't tried on his own. He loved them. Aerobatics suited his cavalier personality.

Emmy-Lou spun obediently under the right conditions. Tim would hold the control wheel all the way back, and apply full rudder just before the stall. The old girl spun tighter to the left, but that may have been her own crooked pedigree. "Tighter" in this case was relative. She would flop over ever so slowly like the last cowboy to die in a movie gunfight. Tim would hang on, gleefully watching the ground rotate ever faster in the windshield.

It wasn't as much fun for the passenger. I crossed my fingers and toes, and imagined bad things happening to the sagging fabric.

"Okay, Tim, that's enough," I would command, "recover now."

"Soon," he would say, and do nothing.

"We're getting too low, Tim!" I'd yell.

"Okay, in a minute," he'd answer.

"No, not 'in a minute,' I'm the instructor, recover now!"

"Okay, okay."

When Tim's dual time reached 12 hours, I booked his flight test. As Chief Flying Instructor at Pie Flying Service, I was the Department of Transport Flight Test Examiner designated for the area. The procedure was to schedule the test and notify the government. The Transport Standards Inspectors held the option of arriving on the appointed day and conducting the test themselves. It was their method of spot checking the flying school's standards. I was afraid if they saw Emmy-Lou and heard the whole story behind Tim's flying background, they would have grounded him, her, Stefan and I, and maybe the whole flying school. They didn't come.

Tim was well behaved during most of the test. We started with a cross-country departure. He worked the computer for accurate speed, time and fuel figures. Then he demonstrated his usual high proficiency in the climbs, descents, turns, and stalls. I asked him to spin the airplane and recover on command, which he did without question. He was consistently scoring five out of five on each manoeuver. It was getting boring.

After the spin, I reduced the power on the Chief's engine and requested a forced approach demonstration down to 500 feet. I hadn't left him much altitude to work with, remembering the airplane's ability to stay in the air.

"Okay, I would land in that field over there," Tim declared, pointing to the right.

He then went through the routine of checking the carburettor heat, throttle, ignition and fuel for a possible cause of an engine failure. He briefed me on what he was doing. I was about to check off another score of five when I realized we weren't headed for the selected field any longer. Tim was concentrating on something to our left. I leaned forward to follow his line of sight. There was a horse-drawn Mennonite buggy on the road on Tim's side. We were turning toward it. Tim was grinning mischieviously.

"Don't do it, Tim!" I shouted.

"We could be landing on that road with an engine failure," he answered hopefully.

"You have to make the original field," I declared.

"It'll be fun," he said.

"I'll fail you for sure," I barked.

"Would you really?" he was stalling for time and still heading for the buggy. We were getting close to 500 feet.

"I'll make sure you never get a pilot licence," I replied sternly. I didn't have that authority, but I made it sound like I did.

At the last possible second, Tim flipped Emmy-Lou into a turn the other way, demonstrating that he could have made the first field.

I don't think the buggy occupants ever saw us, but it made me wonder what Tim did during his solo practise flights. I imagined the local Mennonites had learned to check the skies before pulling onto a road since Tim had moved into the area.

33/ Derry Bound

One day in June I returned from a flight to find Susan bundling Hector's mountain of maps.

"No, no, you don't send the whole map back for renewal," I said. "You cut off the corner that shows the date and return that. It saves postage. We give the rest of the map to the high school for geography classes."

"Not this time boss," Susan replied. She had a bad-news look on her face. "The Canada Map office regrets to inform you that it has changed the format of its aeronautical charts. Starting now, the maps will be printed on both sides with new colouring and symbols to conform with the United States. Each map dealer gets one free copy."

I was devastated. The amount of money involved was not that significant. It was a token devastation. The huge inventory of maps was a legacy left by Hector. To me, they were a symbol of his ineptness, and selling them at a large profit was a symbol of my ability to manage the school better.

"Maybe we can sell the old ones for a few more months without telling the customers they're out of date?" I suggested weakly.

"I have a more positive idea," Susan said. "The new format is a good excuse to send out another newsletter. We'll advertise a special one-night ground school and sell everyone a new map. You can explain the differences and promote the activities we're planning for the summer. What do you think?"

I was having trouble sharing her enthusiasm, but it was a good idea. "Okay," I said. "order 100 new maps and pick a date."

She did and it was a moderate success. Our college customers were long gone, but 20 local pilots came and turned the evening into a season ending social gathering. They each bought a map, but they made it plain they were too busy for summer recreation flying or advanced ground school classes.

John Torrance dropped by the next day. He had attended the map upgrading class. "That was a good session you ran last night," he said. We were sitting in the back office with the door closed at his request.

"You have some good ideas like that, but I think it was obvious the flying activity is going to continue to drop." The flying school owner spoke in his normal quiet voice, but I knew he was building up to something that I didn't want to hear.

"You're right, but I don't know what to do about it. I've tried everything."

"I know and I appreciate it. Don't blame yourself, this happens every year, just when you think everyone in Pie has given up flying, the fall rolls around and everyone comes back."

"I though I could make a difference."

"Well, you have. The school is well run. All we have to do is keep it in good shape to weather the slow summer and be ready for the fall. This is the second month you've operated at a loss. May I suggest you drop some of your advertising and mailing costs, and consider putting Jethro on part-time. He has his military pension to draw on. Do you think he'd mind?"

John was being diplomatic by making "suggestions" and asking questions instead of issuing orders. He was right, but I appreciated the way he presented the inevitable. He was a gentleman.

"I agree. I'll cut the costs and talk to Jethro. Thanks for your support this far."

"You've worked hard," he said, rising out of his chair, "but we can't get blood out of a stone."

Getting through the summer was the immediate problem, but I didn't speak to Jethro right away. I had something else on my mind. The larger issue for me was whether I wanted to coast through summer only to become second fiddle to Hector in the fall. The Pie in the Sky job had been useful until now, but I had to think of what I was going to do with my career over the long term.

I called Larry, my flying friend from years ago who had declined joining me at Pie. He had airline aspirations and was working for a flying school/charter operator in Derry, a good sized town in Central Ontario. Derry Air owned twin-engined aircraft.

"Hello, Larry?"

"It's your good buddy here. How're you doing?"

"Great. How's the job going?"

"Good. Yeah, I'm still flogging the flying school at Pie."

"Well, to tell you the truth, things are a little slow. I was wondering if Derry Air was looking for a top-notch instructor?"

"You think so? Good."

"Yeah, I'll give the owner a call."

"Irving Mingy, okay, thanks Larry. I really appreciate this."

That night I suggested to Susan that I try to get an interview for an instructing job in Derry.

"Yes!" she exclaimed immediately.

"Yes? — no ifs, ands, or buts? — no discussion?"

"None whatsoever." The set of her jaw indicated that it had been decided before I had made the suggestion. I'd seen the look before. Susan wanted a change.

"I didn't know we were so close to moving," I said.

"You do now."

"You should have said something."

"I was close, but you were doing your own thing and I didn't want to spoil that. Now I think it's time you went to Derry and do whatever it takes to get hired. It's a large town and I'll be able to land a job in ladieswear."

"No more flying school receptionist?" I was teasing her and she knew it.

"Aircraft calling Pie," she announced, pretending to hold a microphone. "there's no traffic in the area, it's time to move on."

"Roger," I said.

34/ Pie In The Sky

Irving Mingy was making money with Derry Air. The secret of his success was a vicious cheapness that would have embarrassed Robbie Burns. But I didn't know any of this when I was at Pie In The Sky. My friend Larry had told me that instructors at the Derry Air flying school could work their way into the charter department and fly twin-engine aircraft. It sounded attractive. There had to be more to aviation than riding around Pie in Cessna 150s.

With Larry's encouragement, I phoned Mingy. The Derry Air owner didn't sound excited by my call, but agreed to see me.

On my next day off, I drove to Derry. The airport was another ex-World War II training field, but unlike Pie it appeared to be a hive of aviation activity. Five large hangars lined the ramp and there were airplanes parked in front of each one. A couple of small regional airliners were nosed up to a terminal building.

I found the Derry Air hangar and walked into the office. There was a receptionist squatting on a stool behind the flight desk. I felt sorry for the stool. The middle-aged woman would have made a good fat lady in the circus. Her large frame was draped in a tent dress. Her puffy face was liberally punctuated with warts and topped with unruly hair.

I put on my best smile and approached the desk. "Hello," I said. "I have an appointment with Mr. Mingy this morning."

She looked at me, but didn't say anything. I felt that I was being silently interviewed on the spot.

"You got a name?" she finally asked. Her tone matched her neutral expression.

I told her who I was.

She turned in the direction of an open door behind her and, without raising her voice, said, "He's here."

There was no reply. "Go on in," she said.

"Thank you," I replied.

I walked around the counter and approached the door. Inside was a small, bare office. A lean, casually dressed man was sitting behind a desk, reading a ledger.

"Come in," he said without looking up. "Leave the door open." His voice was almost a whisper. His face was badly scarred. He looked like an aging welterweight boxer with a losing record.

He lifted his head and said, "Why do you want you to work here?" The question came straight out. There was no, "How do you do? I'm Irving Mingy," or "Pleased to meet you." He stared at me while waiting for a reply.

I was in a dilemma. Mingy looked like he could spot a lie a mile away, but I couldn't tell him the truth. I couldn't say I wanted to rape his flying school for twin-engine flying time in order to bag a Multi-Engine Rating and jump to his charter department. I swallowed hard and launched into my prepared speech. "I'd like to join your operation for the opportunity to earn more revenue. At the small school where I work now, I only get four or five hours of revenue flying a day and at that I'm just warming up." I paused to let that sink in.

Mingy clenched his teeth and flexed his facial scars. "That's bullshit," he said. He was right, but it wasn't the reply I was expecting. "If you want to teach here to get some multi-engine time and move on, that's fine, but if you're going to spin tales, go somewhere else."

That killed the rest of my speech. If he wasn't impressed by my revenue capacity, then he wouldn't be interested in my ideas on how to run a flying school. "I'll work," I said.

"Good. Same terms as everyone else," he replied. "eight dollars per revenue hour, payable at the end of the following month."

I did a quick mental calculation: five revenue hours per good day and 200 "good days" a year (optimistically) added up to $8,000. It wasn't bad; about the same as I was already making. Mingy was charging $12 an hour for his instructors' time, but he'd have to pay benefits out of that.

"All my pilots work on contract," he continued. "Set up your own company and bill me for services rendered, just like a plumber. That way you look after your own benefits and insurance. It saves me a lot of paperwork."

It saved him a lot of money too. With holiday pay and minimum benefits, the $8 an hour would have been $10. Now it was effectively much less.

"If you want to train on the Twin Comanche," he said, "it's available to staff for $45 an hour."

Now the man was talking my language. I would need about 20 hours in that airplane to get a Multi-Engine Instrument Rating. Mingy had just saved me $300.

"Between midnight and six in the morning," he added.

I was beginning to realize that I was talking to a real tightwad. I was pleased to have impressed him enough to land a job, but I was less sure that working at Derry Air would be a good idea. Next I expected the owner to charge me for parking my car. I was close.

"Tell Doris you're going to start in a week and give her $20 for a month's coffee fund."

That was it; I finally spoke up. "I don't drink coffee, and I have to give my employer notice." It was a weak protest.

"The coffee's for the customers and I've already spoken to John Torrance," Mingy said.

I fought to keep my jaw from dropping to the floor. I hadn't mentioned anything to John about leaving Pie In The Sky. Mingy was way ahead of me.

"He said you're a good instructor," the Derry Air owner continued. "I hope you prove him right. Leave the door open on the way out."

The interview was over. I could tell him to jump in the lake or I could thank him and leave.

"I'll do my best, sir," I said. He went back to studying his ledger. I turned and walked out.

I went around to the front of the counter and approached the receptionist. "Hi. Mr. Mingy asked me to tell you I'm going to start instructing here in a week."

"You got twenty bucks?" she asked.

"No," I replied. It was the truth, but I might have said it anyway. Between Attilla in the office and Godzilla behind the counter, I was having many second thoughts about working at Derry Air.

"Bring it with you next time," she said. "A week today is next Thursday," she added and then looked at me expectantly.

"Yes," I said, looking just as expectantly.

"Bad day," she said. "Two airplanes are booked off for maintenance. Start a week tommorrow. That's a Friday."

Apparently Derry Air was owned by Mingy, but was run from the stool. "Okay, a week tomorrow," I said.

"Right, Friday."

Before I turned to go, Doris leaned over and said in a lowered tone, "The coffee money is Mr. Mingy's funny way of making you part of the team. Bring it on Friday and he won't ask for it again."

Her expression remained neutral, but, behind the bushy eyebrows, the multiple chins and the warts, I thought I detected a hint of kindness.

"All right, thanks for the tip," I said.

145

I departed shaking my head. Derry Air was a different place. I wasn't sure if I wanted to work there or not.

I walked outside into the early summer sunshine and saw my friend Larry doing a walkaround inspection with a student on a Twin Comanche. The sleek little aircraft sat on the ramp in a rakish stance. Together the engines produced triple the horsepower of a Cessna 150. The airplane's shark-like nacelles and pointed nose made it look fast even on the ground. I thought it would be fun to fly.

Beside the hangar two mechanics were installing the cowlings on a Piper Navajo. This eight-passenger, twin-engined aircraft had six times the power of a Cessna 150. I walked over.

"Mind if I have a look?" I asked the nearest mechanic.

"No, help yourself."

"Thank you."

I leaned in at the airstair door and peered forward. It was a cabin class airplane with a narrow isle between the seats. The leather upholstery and woodgrain paneling looked rich. I could only see the copilot's side of the cockpit, but there were more radios and instruments than I had ever seen before.

I left Derry Air with my mind made up. I'd work for Attilla.

Susan was ecstatic. She had mentally moved out of Pie since I had first suggested it. "No more clodhoppers and no more log books," she exclaimed.

"Yeah," I agreed, "but it still bothers me that Hector could make a profit with that place and I couldn't."

"Well, you know Hector doesn't run it on good business sense, so don't let it bother you."

"So why was he successful and I wasn't?"

"I don't know, but don't worry about it. Chalk it up to pie in the sky."

Enjoy other books by Garth Wallace

"Fly Yellow Side Up"

This is the humorous story of a suburban flying instructor who moves up north to seek the freedom and glory of bush flying. It is the ideal situation for a city slicker to make a fool of himself. You won't be disappointed.

"Blue Collar Pilots"

"Blue Collar Pilots" is a lighthearted tribute to the real pilots in aviation, the low-profile cockpit grunts who don't fly airplanes that fly themselves. The book is a collection of one-liners, jokes and anecdotes that celebrate the rough and tumble blue collar pilots.

"Don't Call Me a Legend"

Charlie Vaughn is Canada's most famous modern day aviator. This biography is a legacy of aviation stories about Vaughn working his way from flying farm boy to world renowned ferry pilot.

"Derry Air"

In "Derry Air", flying instructor Wallace meets the wonderfully sarcastic ground school instructor, Dutch, linecrew Huey, Duey and Louey, a horse that flies and the most odd-ball collection of student pilots ever assembled at one flying school. "Derry Air" is aviation humor in the best Wallace style.

All of Wallace's books are available at pilot supply shops, better book stores or directly from the publisher:

Happy Landings
RR # 4
Merrickville, Ontario
Canada, K0G 1N0

Tel.: 613-269-2552
Fax: 613-269-3962
Web site: www.happylanding.com
E-mail: books@happylanding.com

ABOUT THE AUTHOR

Garth Wallace
Aviator /Author /Publisher /Speaker /Humorist

Aviator
Garth Wallace never intended to be a humor writer. "I wanted to fly, but I always enjoyed a funny story." Wallace is originally from St. Catharines, Ontario where he learned to fly in a Fleet Canuck in 1966. He followed his dream into an aviation career. "I flew as an instructor, bush pilot, charter pilot and corporate pilot, and enjoyed every minute of it."

Author
It was during his flying career that Wallace met the crazy characters and lived the humorous stories that are in his books. He started writing about the more interesting people in aviation with just-for-fun articles in local flying school newsletters and then national aviation magazines. Now there are five books by Wallace.

Publisher
Wallace is the publisher of Canadian Flight, a monthly newspaper which is the voice of the 17,000-member Canadian Owners and Pilots Association. He lives outside of Ottawa, Ontario with his wife and book publisher Liz Wallace and their American Trainer.

Speaker/Humorist
Wallace is available to aviation organizations seeking an informed but entertaining guest speaker. For more information, contact Happy Landings.

Happy Landings
RR 4, Merrickville, Ontario
Canada K0G 1N0

Tel.: 613-269-2552
Fax: 613-269-3962
Web site: www.happylanding.com
E-mail the author: garth@happylanding.com